THE ROYAL DOCTOR'S BRIDE

BY
JESSICA MATTHEWS

 **MILLS & BOON®**

First published in Great Britain 2008
Large Print edition 2009
Harlequin Mills & Boon Limited,
Eton House, 18-24 Paradise Road,
Richmond, Surrey TW9 1SR

© Jessica Matthews 2008

ISBN: 978 0 263 20528 2

Set in Times Roman 16¼ on 18½ pt.
17-0809-51833

Harlequin Mills & Boon policy is to use papers that are
natural, renewable and recyclable products and made
from wood grown in sustainable forests. The logging and
manufacturing process conform to the legal environmental
regulations of the country of origin.

Printed and bound in Great Britain
by CPI Antony Rowe, Chippenham, Wiltshire

The screen had gone dark, but she was still reeling from what she had seen and heard. "I thought you were exaggerating," she admitted. "But you weren't, were you?"

He shook his head, then sat down. "No."

She faced him. "According to the reporter, no one in authority has a solution. What do you think I can do?"

"The experts believe a more 'personal' solution between our families is required." The corners of his mouth turned up slightly. "They're hoping to tie the two royal houses together."

"How would you tie two royal houses...?" Her voice died as she realized exactly the sort of "personal" relationship he wanted. "You can't possibly be thinking of—"

He finished her sentence. "Marriage."

Marriage.

The word echoed in her head.

Marriage.

To a man she'd only met earlier in the day.

After years of working in the ER, she'd always considered herself unshockable, but the word definitely shifted the ground underneath her. "We're supposed to get married?" she managed to croak.

He leaned forward and rested his elbows on his knees. "Yes."

Her heart pounded and an urge to escape swept over her. "This is a joke, right?"

"Not at all."

Jessica Matthews's interest in medicine began at a young age, and she nourished it with medical stories and hospital-based television programmes. After a stint as a teenage candy-striper, she pursued a career as a clinical laboratory scientist. When not writing or on duty she fills her day with countless family and school-related activities. Jessica lives in the central United States with her husband, daughter and son.

Recent titles by the same author:

HIS LONG-AWAITED BRIDE

THE ROYAL DOCTOR'S BRIDE

To everyone who ever pretended to be a princess.
I hope you all found your prince…

CHAPTER ONE

"DR SUTTON, we have a problem."

In the process of jotting down a script and mentally calculating a drug dosage for her patient, Gina Sutton answered absent-mindedly, "I'll be right there."

"This can't wait too long," Nurse Lucy Fields urged.

A warning note in her tone pulled Gina's attention away from her task. She glanced at the normally unflappable woman and saw the distress written all over her face. While the unusual was the norm in Belmont Memorial's Emergency Department, something had upset their nursing supervisor.

"Noted," she said calmly, before turning back to her patient, forty-year-old Jim Pearce. "According to the X-rays, you've sprained, not broken, your wrist. You'll need to keep it immobilized for several weeks to give the muscles time to recover. Here's a prescription…" she tore off the sheet "…for an anti-inflammatory. Take as directed. And if your wrist isn't better in a few weeks, either come back or visit your family doctor. Any questions?"

Jim shook his head.

"Just remember, no more hammering or heavy lifting in the meantime," she cautioned. "Wearing a splint for support doesn't mean you can do everything you did before. If you don't give yourself time to heal, you'll have worse problems."

His face colored slightly, as if she'd read his mind and knew his intent. "OK. A few weeks is all, right?"

"At least three, maybe more."

"Doctor," Lucy urged from the door.

Telling her patient goodbye, Gina followed Lucy into the hallway. "What's the big problem that couldn't wait two more minutes?"

"It's Dr Nevins. He's gone *crazy*!"

"What's he done now?" Gina asked tiredly, already wondering what mistake she'd have to correct this time. Bill Nevins may be the Director of Emergency Services, but an intern could do a better job. On the few occasions when he assisted with a trauma, he was usually more hindrance than help. If he didn't have connections, she believed, he wouldn't have been hired in the first place.

"The man has completely lost his sanity," Lucy declared. "He's storming around his office and when I tried to go inside, he threw his glass paperweight at me!"

"He's always been high-strung," Gina soothed. "What upset him today?"

"I don't know, but he was fine until he got a phone call. You have to talk to him, Gina. You're the only one in the entire department he'll listen to."

For some reason, during the two years she'd been in Belmont's ER, she'd always been able to reason with the man, even when he was at his most unreasonable. When he'd wanted to fire a nurse for dropping a syringe during a code blue, she'd convinced him to give the poor girl a second chance. When he refused to spend the money to replace their defibrillator, she'd calmly reminded him of how costly a potential lawsuit would be, not to mention how his reputation would suffer.

Now, apparently, her negotiation skills would be needed once again to deal with his latest temper tantrum.

"All right," Gina said resignedly, as she handed over Jim Pearson's chart and tucked her pen into the breast pocket of her lab coat. "Let's beard the lion in his den."

To her surprise, his door stood open and she cautiously walked in, noticing how the normally neat office now looked as if a tornado had whirled through. Papers and medical books covered the floor, boxes stood on top of Bill's desk, and file drawers were yanked off their tracks. Even the philodendron she'd brought to soften the stark white walls lay on its side, dirt spilling out of the pot across the top of the filing cabinet.

"What's up?" she asked calmly as she righted the plant.

Bill paused from riffling through the papers on his desk. "I've been fired, that's what."

It's about time, she thought. "Really?" she asked, trying to sound horrified but certain she failed miserably. "Whatever for?"

He waved aside her question. "The reasons don't matter. The point is, I've given my all to this place, and this is how they repay me."

Privately, Gina wondered how a man who worked three, maybe four hours a day could claim "he'd given his all", but it wasn't her place to argue. Her goal now was to bring calm to a potentially unstable situation.

"What happens now?" she asked, more concerned about the repercussions to their department rather than to Bill's professional life.

He waved furiously at the wall clock. "Who knows? I have thirty minutes to pack up and get out. *Thirty minutes*," he ranted. "After ten years of unfailing service, struggling to operate on the shoestring budget they gave me…well, it's unthinkable and insulting!" He grabbed his coffee-mug, then hefted it in his hand. In the next breath, he heaved it at the metal filing cabinet.

Gina didn't have time to dodge before the ceramic cup shattered into a hundred pieces. A sharp sting bit into her cheek and she instinctively touched her face. No real damage as far as she could tell. Although she was somewhat disconcerted because Bill had never injured anyone before during one of his tirades, the burden of restoring his reason clearly fell to her.

She ignored the lingering discomfort and began in her most placating tone, "Now, Bill—"

She didn't get past his name before a tall, dark-haired man burst into the office, wearing an expensively tailored dark gray suit and a grim expression.

"Throw one more thing and you'll be flying

through the air, too," he snarled as he moved in front of her, effectively blocking her from her irate superior. In the next instant, he whipped out a snowy white handkerchief and pressed it into her hand. "You'd better take care of that, Gina."

Too curious about the scene unfolding, especially when two more men arrived who were more stocky and not quite as tall or as handsome, she didn't ask how this stranger knew her name. She simply nodded and did as she was told.

To her surprise, a large smear of blood—*her* blood—stained the expensive cotton square. Quickly, she pressed it to her cheek again, more curious about the drama than about her scratch, especially when her rescuer approached Bill behind his desk.

"You, Dr Nevins," the authoritative man accused in a deep, stern voice, "have forfeited your right to collect your things. Leave the premises immediately."

Bill straightened to his full five feet five inches and his beady little eyes narrowed. "Who are *you* to tell *me* what I can and cannot do?"

"I'm your replacement," the fellow stated calmly and firmly. "Goodbye, Dr Nevins."

He raised one hand and in the blink of an eye

the two men moved round the desk from opposite directions to grab Bill's arms and lead him toward the door.

"But I didn't hurt her on purpose," Bill screeched. "Tell him, Gina."

Everyone's gaze landed on Gina. "Bill wouldn't hurt me," Gina responded. "Not intentionally."

Her handsome knight folded his arms and regarded her cooly. "A man with such an obvious lack of control can't be trusted."

"You can't do this," Bill shouted. "I have thirty minutes left."

Bill's replacement, with his regal bearing and handsomely aristocratic features, looked down his aquiline nose. "You now have none. Take him away."

"But my things," Bill wailed over his shoulder as the two henchmen literally lifted him off the ground.

"Dr Sutton will ship your personal possessions to you." And with that, the two apparent security guards carried him out, kicking and screaming.

Gina stared at the now empty doorway. "At the risk of sounding completely ridiculous, what just happened?"

"Changing of the guard," the man said as he

stood in front of her. "Let me look at that." Without waiting for her permission, he tipped her chin upward, pulled away the handkerchief and peered at her face.

Strangely enough, an attack of self-conscious-ness swept over Gina. The most handsome man she'd seen in ages had burst into her department like an avenging angel and now was studying her face as if he'd never seen a scratch before.

"It's nothing," she said inanely, extremely con-scious of two things—his six-foot-plus frame, which made her feel petite at five foot eight, and a delightfully masculine scent that made her ap-preciate being a female.

He pressed on her cheekbone and frowned. "You need a stitch."

"I don't think so."

He raised both eyebrows, eyebrows framing chocolate brown eyes that were deep, dark pools. "Are you questioning my medical judgement?"

"I believe so. Yes."

A huge grin spread across his face. The dazzling brilliance of his smile made him seem younger, more approachable, and less formidable.

"At least you're honest," he said.

"It's the best policy," she answered.

"Have a seat," he ordered. "I'll be right back."

She might have obeyed, but it wasn't in her nature to ignore the obvious. Because she weighed her problems more easily if she was busy, she carefully picked up the shattered remnants of Bill's mug while she contemplated the sharp turn that the morning had taken.

Bill was gone. While she took a few seconds to rejoice, she knew life in Belmont's ER might not turn out better than it had been under Bill's administration. Clearly, his successor—whoever he was—had a definite take-charge attitude. Once he'd plotted his course of action, he followed it, which was a good thing provided he based his decisions upon facts and logic. But if he didn't, they would be in trouble, because she doubted if she'd be as successful at negotiating with him as she had been with Bill.

No matter. She'd learned the art of persuasion at a young age and had developed it fully as she had taken care of her father near the end of his too-short life. She hadn't met a man yet who came close to Arthur John Sutton in stubbornness.

With any luck, however, the new ED Director would be more reasonable than Bill, although after watching him mercilessly throw Bill out of the department, she hoped he didn't normally manage his subordinates with the same dictatorial style.

"I see you're a person who doesn't follow orders," he said behind her a minute later.

"I follow them when they're rational," she replied pertly.

"Do I detect shades of a warning?"

"If the shoe fits." She dumped the last shard of china in the trash can. "I thought I'd get a head start on cleaning up the mess."

"I appreciate the offer, but someone can take care of it later."

She eyed the piles of papers and hesitated, but when he added, "Please," she couldn't disobey.

He cleared off a corner of the desk with one swipe of his hand, then placed a bottle of alcohol, several sterile gauze squares and a suture kit on the surface before he faced her. "Don't worry. Rational is my middle name. Are you ready?"

She eyed his supplies. "You don't stitch a scratch. It's hardly bleeding now anyway."

He whipped a small mirror out of his pocket. "See for yourself."

Her reflection revealed a large drop of blood

that welled up in the cut which was dangerously close to her right eye. "No stitches," she insisted.

"If you're worried about my sewing ability…"

"Your abilities aren't in question. I simply don't think it's necessary."

He perched on the edge of the desk. "I'll call a plastic surgeon, then. We'll get his opinion."

"You will do no such thing," she stated firmly. "A butterfly bandage will do the job. You're over-reacting. So the cut is a little deep. One stitch isn't worth the trouble."

"You'll have a scar," he warned.

She eyed the cut before she dabbed the blood away. "Probably, but it won't be so big that make-up won't cover it." She grinned as she handed the mirror back. "It will blend in with the normal wrinkles. No one will ever notice."

"Your significant other might."

"If he can't look past a hairline scar, then he won't be my significant other, will he?" she asked lightly. "Would it bother you if *your* significant other had a scar on her face?"

"Of course not." He appeared affronted.

She smiled. "Then I rest my case."

He hesitated for a heartbeat. "I can't talk you into this, can I?"

"Nope. Not a chance. As a patient, I have the right to refuse or accept treatment."

"OK. Butterfly bandage it is." He rose to shrug off his jacket, revealing a white shirt that covered deliciously wide shoulders.

"And I'll take care of it myself."

He poured alcohol on a gauze pad. "I'm sure you can, but you aren't. This is going to sting a bit."

She nearly howled as he pressed the saturated pad to her face and disinfected the wound, but she bit back her yelp. To take her mind off the burning sensation, she concentrated on him.

Whoever he was, he was too handsome, too well built, too *everything* for words. His short hair was the color of dark molasses and seemed just as thick. His features reflected an aristocratic heritage and his long eyelashes were every woman's dream.

As he probed and prodded, she noticed his long fingers and light touch. Idly, she wondered how he'd look in a scrub suit, and if they could find any lab coats that would fit.

"The man should be drawn and quartered," he muttered as he ripped open another package of gauze.

"Who, Bill?"

"Who else?"

"He's harmless. Incompetent but, overall, harmless."

"From where I'm standing, I'd disagree."

Perhaps he was right. The room was a mess, and he *had* thrown a paperweight at Lucy before he'd pitched his coffee-mug in a fit of pique.

"You shouldn't have gotten in the way," he chided.

"Someone had to talk to him, calm him down. I've done it before. Given a few more minutes, I would have again."

"The diplomat."

She hadn't ever described herself with that term before, but it fit. "At times."

He pulled the butterfly bandage tight to hold the cut edges of her skin together. "Don't get it wet," he informed her.

"Yes, I know. Thank you." She straightened in her chair. "Now, if you don't mind, I'd like a few answers."

He perched against the edge of the desk in front of her. "What do you want to know?"

"Your name, for starters."

His perfect smile was sheepish. "In all the excitement, I left out the formalities, didn't I?"

"Given the circumstances, it was understandable."

"I'm Dr Ruark Thomas, at your service."

She held out her hand. "Pleased to meet you, Dr Thomas. Welcome to Belmont Memorial."

"Thank you."

Gina became instantly aware of two things, the touch of his fingers against hers and his deep voice. Both caused her nerve endings to tingle pleasantly and create a surprisingly powerful attraction that tugged at her middle. She couldn't remember the last time she'd felt more than a glimmer of interest in someone she'd met, but this was certainly not the time for her hormones to kick in or her subconscious to get caught up in the moment. Yet, in spite of her mental scolding, she reluctantly withdrew her hand and forced herself to concentrate.

"You have a lot of ER experience?" she asked.

"Some. I moved here from California, thinking it would be nice to try life in the Great Midwest," he said smoothly. "I trained in Great Britain, specialized in emergency medicine in New York, and spent most of my time over the years with a number of relief agencies."

"Interesting. And now you've come to boring little Belmont Memorial."

He chuckled. "From indications so far, being here will be anything but boring."

The men who'd carried Bill away suddenly appeared in her mind's eye. "And the two men with you?"

"Security guards. You'll probably see Hugh and Joachim a lot in the days ahead. Then again, you may not. They work best behind the scenes, or so I've been told."

The two men certainly outclassed Belmont's regular department security guards. Oscar Burns, who, with an extra fifty pounds around his mid-section, only moved fast when someone brought homemade goodies to share and Hal Jarvis, who, at twenty-four, looked like he was thirteen, and hadn't filled out his gangly teenage frame yet.

In contrast, Hugh and Joachim were profession-als through and through. Their muscles had muscles and a mere glance from those piercing eyes would coax co-operation from the most difficult of patients and visitors. They'd definitely be handy to have around on a Friday or Saturday night.

"Is Dr Lansing afraid Bill will make trouble?" Lansing was the Chief of Medicine and he was the sort who didn't act upon anything until the i's were dotted and t's were all properly crossed.

"It's a possibility."

"Bill is all bluster," she told him. "He won't make trouble if he suspects those two are hanging around. He'll be too embarrassed, especially if he might be hauled outside like a bag of dirty laundry again. Frankly, after what I saw, I'd hate to run into them in a dark alley."

The corners of his mouth twitched. "Stay on Hugh and Joachim's good side and you won't have any problems."

"You're already on a first-name basis?"

"It seemed appropriate."

The dull throb in her cheek demanded a couple of acetaminophen, but she wanted answers more than she wanted a painkiller. "I can't believe Bill's gone. Do you know what prompted his sudden exit?"

"I'm not privy to all the details, but your administration hasn't been happy with the way he's managed this department."

"They actually noticed?"

"Yes, they did."

"When did they decide to take matters into their own hands?"

"Apparently they began making discreet inquiries several months ago. I heard about the position and thought it would be a challenge, so I completed my other commitments and here I am." His face darkened. "However, if I'd known he was such a volatile man, I would have arranged my schedule differently."

She hardly knew what to say, but a warm, fuzzy feeling spread through her. No one, since her father had died, had been so concerned about her safety. What woman wouldn't feel flattered?

"You, on the other hand," he scolded, "shouldn't have gone into his office when he was so upset."

"We've been over this before. I had to go in. There was no one else."

"There is now," he stated firmly. "You won't do anything like that again."

"Are you planning to go ballistic at some point in time, too?" she asked lightly.

He smiled. "No, but one never knows what will happen. You're too valuable to put yourself in harm's way."

Why today's incident bothered Ruark so much she didn't know, other than he didn't want to find a replacement physician. Even so, working in Emergency carried a normal element of risk and danger, especially if one considered some of the situations they handled on Saturday nights. Mentioning a few of those incidents seemed counterproductive, so she changed the subject.

"You're truly taking over the department?" she asked.

"I intended to call a staff meeting as soon as Bill left, but we got sidetracked," he said wryly.

No doubt he referred to tending the scratch on her face. "We can call one now, unless you'd rather tidy your office first."

He glanced around. "From the looks of things, it will take a long time. I'll meet our group instead."

"Good idea. I'd bet they're all dying of curiosity."

A knock at the door interrupted. "Come in," he called out.

Lucy poked her head inside. "Is everything OK in here?"

"It's fine," Gina responded.

"Can I get either of you anything?" she asked. "Coffee, tea, or…?"

"Thank you, but not at the moment," Ruark answered politely.

Disappointment flitted across Lucy's features. "If you should change your mind…"

"We'll let you know," Gina assured her.

"OK." The nurse disappeared and Gina faced

Ruark. "The natives are definitely dying of curiosity."

"I'll deal with them in a minute," he said. "But before I do, I'd like to discuss a more personal matter."

Knowing she had nothing to hide, she shrugged. "Sure."

He studied her intently. "You truly didn't know I was coming?"

"Didn't have a clue," she responded cheerfully.

"My name didn't sound familiar?"

She shook her head. "Should it?"

"Really?"

"Really. Have you been in the news?" She hoped not. If he was a household name and she didn't recognize it, she'd feel horribly awkward.

"Not lately."

She smiled. "Good, because otherwise I'd have to apologize. I rarely watch television," she admitted.

His gaze held hers. "What if I told you I'm originally from Marestonia."

Marestonia? A warning bell sounded in her head and her smile froze in place. *Stay calm*, she told herself. Lots of people lived in Marestonia.

She pretended ignorance. "Someplace in Eastern Europe, isn't it?"

"Next door to Avelogne."

Her heart pounded painfully in her chest. She hadn't heard the name of her father's country since she'd turned sixteen and he'd told her the entire tale of his life.

A life he'd given up rather than sacrifice his principles.

A life where he'd gained a wife and daughter and lost everything else.

"Your father and mine were friends years ago."

The past wasn't supposed to surface after all these years. Her father had left that life behind, never to embrace it again. Acknowledging it now seemed rather disloyal to her parents' memory.

"Was your father an aeronautical engineer, too?" She sounded stiffly polite as she pretended ignorance of her family background. "Did the two of them do business together?"

"Their friendship began long before your father moved to Seattle. *Countess*."

She drew herself up at the title she had a right to use but didn't. "Do *not* call me that."

"Deny your heritage all you want, but I have the proof."

"And what if you do? It means nothing. I don't have any official ties to Avelogne."

"Ah, but you admit you do have ties."

Feeling like a mouse caught in a trap, she bit her lip, reluctant to say anything else.

"You do," he insisted. "You have a grandmother, aunts, uncles and cousins."

"Whom I never met," she countered. "I'm thirty years old and I've lived my entire life without them. I'm not interested in changing my family dynamics now."

With a blinding flash of insight, the pieces of the puzzle making up Ruark Thomas began to align themselves in a picture she didn't like. His aristocratic bearing, his take-charge attitude, his familiarity with the security guards all suggested he was more than a physician, more than the new chief of emergency services.

She studied him with the same intensity she used when searching for bacteria under a microscope. "Who *are* you, Dr Thomas?"

CHAPTER TWO

RUARK watched the woman in front of him. Her green eyes flashed with fire and she bristled with a combination of indignation and suspicion. Breaking the news to her wouldn't be easy; he'd known it for some time, which was why he'd planned and orchestrated the proper timing.

He clicked his heels together and bowed slightly. "Ruark Benjamin Mikael Thomas, Prince of Marestonia."

"Prince?" she asked on a near squeak. "I thought you were a physician."

"They aren't mutually exclusive. I happen to be both."

"What brings a physician slash prince of Marestonia to Belmont Memorial?"

"To work, like everyone else," he promptly answered.

"Since when do princes need to earn a living?"

"It's called serving the people," he said lightly.

"As the third son, I was free to choose my own career, and I chose medicine. Just as your cousin, Leander, did."

Curiosity flashed in her eyes at the mention of a cousin who shared her interest and her profession, but a few seconds later indifference appeared, as if she simply refused to acknowledge any sort of connection between her and her father's family. "And you chose to work in the US?"

"When I'm not involved in relief work."

"How noble."

"Please, feel free to tell me what you *truly* think."

His gentle rebuke brought color to her face. "I apologize," she said stiffly. "As a physician, I was out of line to say something so unforgivable."

"Apology accepted." Gina was many things, but she didn't hesitate to speak her mind, he decided. From the reports he'd read about her, he hadn't expected her to do otherwise.

She crossed her arms. "OK, you're a prince who works for a living, but out of all the hospitals in this country, what made you choose Belmont?"

"Because you're here," he said simply.

She scoffed. "Oh, please. You can't be serious."

"It's true," he insisted. "I came as soon as a job was available."

She looked puzzled. "But why? We don't know each other."

"Your grandmother and my father sent me." He reached into the left inside pocket of his suit coat, retrieved a white envelope and held it out to her. "The Queen Mother asked if I would deliver this."

Recognition flashed in her eyes as her gaze traveled from one corner emblazoned with the royal crest of the House of Avelogne to the middle where her name appeared in large, beautifully precise script. "Why would the royal family send a letter to me?" she asked suspiciously.

"You'll have to read the explanation for yourself."

She eyed the envelope as if it were a pure culture of *Hantavirus*, but indecision flickered across her face. He hoped her curiosity would overrule the hard feelings she so plainly felt.

Reluctantly, she accepted the offering and hefted it in her hand before tapping the long edge against one palm. "If you wanted to be the Queen Mother's errand boy, you didn't have to accept a job at Belmont to do so."

Although amused by her bluntness, he hid a smile. "For the record, your uncle is now King, which makes your grandmother the Queen Mother, but to answer your question, no, I didn't."

"Then why did a Prince of Marestonia, a *Doctor* Prince no less, move here just to deliver her mail?"

"You'll understand when you read what your grandmother has to say."

"If this is a 'hi, how are you' note, I'm not interested," she warned.

"Read it," he repeated. "I'll answer your questions *after* you read the letter."

"All right, I will."

Suspecting she'd leave under the guise of needing privacy and then, when she was alone, she would destroy her grandmother's letter unopened, Ruark positioned himself in front of the room's only exit. "I'll give you all the time you need, without saying a word."

She clutched the envelope until it wrinkled. "I can't deal with this right now."

"Of course you can. You're not afraid, are you?" he asked, hoping she'd respond to the challenge in his voice.

She did. She squared her shoulders and met his gaze as she defiantly slid her finger under the glued flap and pulled out a piece of expensive stationery. "Happy now?" she asked crossly.

"Not until you read it."

"Then stop hovering," she snapped.

Once again, he hid his amusement and moved closer to the door. "Sorry," he said, unapologetically. It was clear she was as irritated with him as she was at her grandmother for breaking years of silence, but a journey began with a single step and Gina had taken hers.

Gina took a deep breath as she unfolded the single sheet. The words written in the same beautiful script as on the envelope jumped off the page.

Greetings, dearest Granddaughter,

We trust this letter finds you well. Although we have never met, we still consider you an integral part of our family.

Gina inwardly scoffed, but read on.

You will never know how much I deeply regret the family differences that have separated us all these years, but I hope you will find it in your heart to put the past behind us and look to the future.

Avelogne needs your help, my dearest Gina. Its alliances with Marestonia are threatened and neither country can afford to lose the goodwill we've enjoyed for centuries. We realize your loyalties do not lie with us, but your parents are at the heart of the matter and I hope you will find it in your heart to honor them by being part of the solution. Prince Ruark shall relay all the details and explanations necessary.

We know our request will come as a great surprise, but your decision will affect countless people. You are a woman who chose a profession because you care about others and we are confident you shall follow your nature and choose the right course of action.

We shall look forward to hearing from you and soon meeting each other face to face.

With best wishes,

Your Grandmother, Juliana

"What does she mean, my parents are at the heart of the matter?" she asked.

"Today's problems are linked to the government's decision to withhold approval for your parents' marriage."

Her father had mentioned something about that, but had glossed over the details. "Sounds to me like the government made its own dilemma, so they can fix it."

"My family was involved, too."

"Then *you* can do whatever it is you need to do, but count me out." She stepped closer and tried to reach around him for the doorknob.

He gripped her arm and didn't budge. "My aunt gave questionable information to the committee which led them to refuse your father's petition to marry your mother."

"You mean, someone *lied*, and they believed her?" No wonder her parents hadn't spoken of those days except in the most general terms. Her dad, especially, must have felt betrayed by his countrymen who'd trusted the testimony of an outsider instead of his own.

"Unfortunately, yes. Now, after all these years, the truth has come out and tensions are running high. The fate of our nations depends on us."

If not for one woman's pettiness, her entire life might have been different…she might have grown up as a member of a royal family, with doting aunts and uncles, cousins, grandparents marking every major event in her life, sharing in her triumphs and failures, and, most importantly, supporting her after her father's death.

But even if Ruark's aunt had been involved, the decision ultimately rested upon the members of

Parliament. In her opinion, they were as much at fault as Ruark's relative, if not more so.

As she'd already pointed out, it was too late to change the past. Neither was it her responsibility. One thing, however, was certain. She didn't count gullibility among her faults.

"Oh, puhleeze," she scoffed. "Fates of two countries. You can't be serious."

"I am."

According to the grim set to his jaw, he was. "Why would I want to help the same government who carelessly changed my family's life?" she asked.

"Avelogne is your heritage," he said simply. "You also hold dual citizenship, which means you have a legal as well as a moral obligation to Avelogne." He paused. "Do you honestly believe your father wouldn't want you to help his homeland avert a crisis?"

Admittedly, her dad had stayed abreast of all the happenings across the Atlantic. Their home had been littered with newspapers and magazines from various cities. In later years, those had given way to Internet news and emails. Arthur Sutton may not have been in close physical proximity to the land of his birth, but his heart had never left.

"This is quite melodramatic, wouldn't you say?" she asked, struggling to shore up her wavering resolve. "Avelogne and Marestonia losing centuries-old goodwill over a thirty-year-old incident that most don't remember."

"The past hasn't been forgotten," he assured her. "The people of Avelogne lost a favored prince and demand restitution for your parents going into exile. If not, they plan to break off all ties with Marestonia."

She crossed her arms. "So?"

"Each country provides goods and services to the other, which makes them somewhat trade-dependent. This includes everything from agriculture to military technology. If ties are broken, thousands of jobs on both sides of the border will be lost and the economic impact will be huge. It will take years to recover. Meanwhile, people will lose their homes and businesses, farmers won't have an accessible market for their products, children will go hungry. The list goes on."

She'd treated patients who couldn't scrounge together enough money for bus fare, much less their medication. She'd lost track of the number of families she'd fed, either in the cafeteria or a nearby restaurant. As much as she wanted to help them all, she couldn't take responsibility for everyone who walked through Belmont's doors.

"I sympathize with your situation, but the last time I checked, my credentials were limited to medicine, not détente. You'll have to ask someone else."

"There *is* no one else to ask. You're my only option."

"I'm sorry, but my answer is still no." She tried to nudge him aside, but he didn't budge.

"You're a coward."

She stared at him, incredulous. "Because I choose not to immerse myself in the politics that sent my father away from the home he loved, I'm a coward?"

"You don't even know what we're asking," he accused. "The least you can do is listen to the unabridged story before you decide. Refusing to do that is either a show of cowardice or being self-centered. Take your pick."

For a terse moment, the silence became so complete, only the distant ringing of a telephone could be heard.

"I'm sorry Avelogne and Marestonia are suffering a diplomatic crisis," she said quietly. "But I'm just an average woman on the street, so to speak.

I work in a hospital in a relatively bad part of town and deal with drug addicts and gang members on a daily basis. I don't know what you or my grandmother think I can accomplish. I can't undo the past and I don't run in lofty social or political circles of influence, so you're only wasting your time."

"I disagree. You are not an 'average' woman. If you re-established ties with your family, you would enter influential circles," he pointed out. "You are, after all, a countess."

"What if I like my life the way it is? I don't *want* to be known as *Countess*. Anonymity suits me just fine."

"You can remain anonymous and still become reacquainted with your family. The point is, life is too short to bear grudges."

Thinking of her father, who'd died as much from heartache as heart disease, Gina's eyes burned with unexpected moisture.

"Aren't you the least bit interested in hearing their side of the story?" he coaxed, as if hoping curiosity would sway her.

"Will it change anything?" she demanded. "Rewrite the past? Restore my father to the family he loved? Take away my mother's sorrow and guilt for causing him to choose between her and his family? I think not."

"I agree those wrongs can't be undone, but we have to resolve this crisis."

"I don't have to do anything," she retorted, blinking away her unshed tears. "My father left Avelogne and his family long ago. I don't intend to get involved with either now."

He fell silent for a moment, then nodded slowly. "If you don't want to deal with the royal family, you don't have to."

"I don't?"

He shook his head. "The real solution lies between the two of us anyway."

She stared at him, puzzled. "You've lost me."

"While it would help matters if Avelogne could show the world a reunited royal house—namely that Arthur's daughter has been reinstated into the fold—it isn't required. Your relationship with me is the important thing."

"Because of your aunt?" she guessed.

"Yes. On behalf of my entire family, I'd like to apologize for her selfish actions."

She tapped one foot on the floor. "What exactly *was* her motive for ruining my parents' lives?"

He didn't comment, although he heaved a

great sigh. "Margret fell in love with your father and believed that if your mother, Lizbet, disappeared from the scene, she would be able to earn Arthur's affections." He paused. "She was quite shocked when he relinquished his claim to the throne and moved to America. The situation didn't play out quite as she'd planned."

"I'll say," she said wryly. "Whatever her reasons, though, I don't hold you responsible. Neither the past nor your royal connections will interfere with our employer-employee status. As far as I'm concerned, we're simply two physicians who happen to work together in the same department, in the same hospital. So you can call whomever you need to and announce the good news. Then life for everyone can return to normal."

He smiled, as if she'd amused him with her simplistic solution. "It's a start, but, as I've already said, your people demand more than an apology. They want their prince back."

Do you hear that, Dad? A pain shot through her heart. If only he'd lived long enough to see this day. "Impossible," she said flatly.

He nodded. "Which is why the situation is complicated."

"I was afraid you would say that," she said dryly. "But, complicated or not, I can't help you."

He started to speak, but the door edged open and Lucy poked her head inside.

"We're getting a couple of traumas in about five minutes. Two stabbing victims."

Gina had never been so relieved to have patients coming into the ED before. She could deal with medical situations far better than she could sort out diplomatic problems of countries she'd only seen on the map and in occasional family photos.

"Thanks, Lucy," she said. "We'll be right there."

Lucy vanished, apparently without noticing the tension in the office. From the look on Ruark's face, he was clearly glad for the reprieve as well.

"We'll discuss this further tonight," he said. "When we won't be interrupted or distracted."

"There isn't anything to discuss," she protested.

"You need to hear everything," he insisted. "The least you can do is listen."

She wanted to refuse but, after seeing the fierce determination on his face, she knew he wouldn't give up.

She faced him squarely. "OK, but in the meantime you will not breathe a syllable of this conversation to *anyone*. No one knows my background and I prefer to keep it that way."

"You have my word," he agreed. Immediately, he opened the door. "After you, Dr Sutton."

Setting aside her host of questions to mentally gear up for her patients, Gina hurried toward the centrally located nurses' station. "Page Frank," she told Ruby, the desk clerk, referring to their surgical resident, Frank Horton.

With the phone tucked under one ear, Ruby mouthed, "I'm already on it." Then she spoke into the receiver. "I don't care where you have to find him, just do it. We need him in the ER, stat!"

Gina rushed into the opposite hallway to check if Trauma Room One was available, and found Ruark following her like a shadow. "What are you doing here? Bill didn't—"

"It's a new day. Bill isn't here any longer," he pointed out. "As I understand the job, I'm supposed to be available for traumas, and here I am."

Only if I need you, she wanted to protest. But then, with two patients coming in and not knowing the condition of either, she might need an extra pair of hands. The only question was, would he function like Bill and be more hindrance than help?

"Afraid I'll find your department doesn't run smoothly?" he asked.

"We run just fine," she defended tartly. "Feel free to observe for yourself." Already dismissing him, she asked no one in particular, "Where's Casey?"

Another nurse scurried past. "Dr Casey left for his dentist appointment ten minutes ago. Remember?"

How could she have forgotten? Of all the days for him to lose a temporary filling. But considering what had happened so far this morning, she would count herself fortunate if a natural disaster didn't occur.

"Dr Powers is supposed to cover, but he can't come until one-thirty." Toby Powers was a physician who was close to retirement and worked two shifts a week.

"Staff problems?" Ruark asked.

"Nothing we can't work around."

The ambulance bay doors near the nurses' station swooshed open and she rushed forward to greet the two paramedics and the gurney carrying her first patient.

"Twenty-five-year-old male with multiple wounds to the chest," one of the paramedics, Tim Abbott, reported. "Open pneumothorax. BP is one ten over sixty-five…"

Gina listened to his recitation as she donned her protective gear, including a face shield, while following the gurney into the trauma room. Not only was the man's blood pressure low and his heart rate increased, but his skin was cold and clammy and he appeared restless in spite of his cervical and thoracic spine immobilization. Tim had already inserted an endotracheal tube in the field, but her patient still struggled to breathe and showed jugular vein distension.

She raised the large bandage covering his bloody chest and saw eight puncture wounds, with the largest one near the heart showing frothy blood. Because air and blood were leaking into his thoracic cavity, his lungs couldn't inflate properly. Her work was cut out for her.

To her surprise, a similarly gowned and gloved Ruark appeared in the room. "I've got it under control," she said as she, Tim, Lucy, another nurse and now Ruark prepared to move her patient from the ambulance gurney to a hospital bed.

"Are you warning me away from your patient, Dr Sutton?" he asked coolly.

She mentally noted that she didn't need to take charge, but old habits were hard to break. While she'd have to defer to him for the time being, she'd maintain a watchful eye until she assured herself that the royal doctor truly knew what he was doing.

"Not at all," she answered. "One, two, three, lift!" On Gina's command, their patient made the transition with minimal jostling. Seconds later, she began barking her orders to the nurses who were busy affixing a pulse oximeter, monitoring the IV and taking over ventilation duties. "Get me a chest tube on the double, a CBC and type and cross-match for four units. Where's Horton?"

Becky answered. "He's not here yet."

"Page him again. If he doesn't answer in the next sixty seconds, page Dr Ahmadi too." Ahmadi was Frank Horton's supervisor.

Gina wiped blood away from the largest and most worrisome puncture and revealed heavily tattooed skin. A closer look at his torso showed her what she'd missed before—his entire body was tattooed with mythical creatures. The detailed dragon which was prominently featured on his left bicep was quite distinctive.

"I see we've gotten another one of Picasso's customers."

"Who?" Ruark asked.

"Pablo Picasso. Pablo's his real name and being a local tattoo artist, he calls his parlor Picasso's," she said as she began to palpate along the man's rib cage to determine the chest tube placement site. "He thought the famous name would give his place some class. We see a lot of his work in here."

"Doesn't say much for his choice of clientele," Ruark remarked.

"Pablo is interested in his art, not in people's lifestyle choices," she defended.

"How did you meet him? I wouldn't think a physician and a tattooist would have much in common."

"He came into the ER with pneumonia when I was an intern and we started to talk about all sorts of things. He invited me to his workplace—he dared me to visit, actually, and I did. His drawings are fantastic."

"Did you pick one for yourself?" Lucy asked.

"Sure did. Lidocaine."

Lucy slapped the required syringe into Gina's hand. "Oh, my gosh. You have a tattoo?"

Conscious of Ruark listening intently, Gina wished she hadn't said a word. Her tattoo was none of his business, even if she wasn't ashamed of it. "Yeah."

"You're kidding."

"Come on, Lucy, it isn't that big a deal," Gina defended.

"Hey, any time you veer off the straight and narrow path of respectability to walk on the wild side, it's interesting," Lucy announced. "So what did you choose, and where is it? Don't keep us in suspense."

"It's a frog," Gina snapped. "On my foot. Scalpel."

"I should have guessed. You collect them, don't you?" Lucy slapped the instrument into her hand.

"Yeah." From the sheer volume of inked skin, Gina suspected her patient took as much pride in his body art as Pablo did, so she made the smallest incision possible to accomplish what had to be done. As she punctured the pleura with a Kelly clamp, blood spurted from the hole.

Working frantically, she hardly noticed the appearance of another nurse, and two more paramedics as they wheeled in a second victim who, like the first, had an IV line established and wore an oxygen mask.

"We've got problems here, Doc," Andy Carter, one of the paramedics, announced.

"Tell me about it," she muttered.

"What's wrong?" Ruark abandoned Gina's patient for the new arrival.

"He's got a pneumothorax and I couldn't

intubate him before we brought him in. I tried, but couldn't get through and I didn't want to waste more time trying in the field."

Gina inserted the tube into her John Doe's chest. Immediately blood filled the line and ran into the attached drainage bag. "Hang on, buddy," she told her patient. "We're taking good care of you."

"Give me an endotrachael tube," Ruark ordered as he moved to the head of his patient's gurney.

Andy glanced between her and Ruark. "Doc?"

"Where's Frank?" she asked no one in particular.

"I asked for an endotrach tube," Ruark ground out. "Must I get one myself?"

Everyone froze, including Gina. "What do you think you're doing?" she asked.

"Trying to save this man's life, if someone will give me a damn tube!" he roared as he stood over the second man, who was audibly rasping for breath.

Immediately, the nurses sprang into action.

Gina exchanged a brief glance with Lucy. Ruark would be furious that no one had instantly obeyed his orders. Apparently her days as staff liaison hadn't ended yet but, in all fairness, what could he expect? No one knew of the official leadership change—it all had happened so fast.

If he'd called his staff meeting instead of springing international problems on her that were beyond her control, none of this would have happened, she thought uncharitably.

"By the way," Gina announced offhandedly as she tended her patient, "I'm afraid none of you have met our new emergency director, Dr Ruark Thomas. In case you haven't figured it out yet, he's replaced Bill."

Under the wary greetings offered by the subdued staff, Gina muttered to Lucy, "Keep an eye on him and signal me if you notice he's in over his head."

Lucy obeyed, quietly trading places with the other nurse.

While Gina finished securing the chest tube with sutures and dressed the wound she'd created, she listened to the quiet conversation over the second gurney.

"We can't get through," Ruark declared. "His larynx is fractured and the upper airway is blocked."

"Then he needs a cricothyroidotomy," she interrupted from across the room. Having worked with her share of unseasoned physicians, she was accustomed to sharing her opinions during the trickier situations. "Can we get by with—?"

Ruark must have read her mind. "Ventilating him with only a needle and catheter is a temporary measure. The surgical method will make it easier for placement of a tracheostomy tube later, which he will definitely need."

"OK. I'll be there in a few seconds." But as she watched the blood pour out of her patient's chest into the drainage bag and heard only muffled heart sounds, she knew she couldn't leave his side.

She hated to ask, but she had no choice. "Can you do it on your own?"

"I'm two steps ahead of you," he answered. "Never fear. I've done this once or twice."

Once or twice? Gina mentally groaned. Yet, for a man with such limited experience, he didn't seem flustered or act out of his depth. And while she was relieved by his calm, matter-of-fact manner, she couldn't squelch the irrational notion that he might need the benefit of her expertise. After all, a patient's life was at stake.

"Find the cricoid cartilage, which is approximately two to three centimeters below the thyroid notch," she instructed. "Once the membrane is exposed, puncture it midline. Be careful of the vocal cords and don't puncture—"

"The back wall of the larynx and enter the esophagus. Yes, Gina, I know, but thanks for the reminder."

He didn't sound upset and wasn't yelling at the nurses for not providing the proper supplies at the exact moment he wanted them, which was a one-eighty-degree change from working alongside Bill. Her fears that he was simply a more polished version of their previous director slowly faded as she listened to his calm voice ask questions and give directions. No, it was obvious she didn't need to review his curriculum vitae—his actions spoke of his abilities far better than a list of positions held ever would. If he could handle his current patient's condition, he was a colleague she could trust.

Within seconds, Ruark's patient's audible symptoms of respiratory stridor disappeared, and with it all of her fears about his medical skills. Suddenly, a burden she hadn't realized she'd been carrying lifted.

"Airway's in," he said, sounding quite pleased. "His pneumothorax is next on the agenda."

The activity on the other side of the room faded into the background as the nurse at her side interrupted with a terse "BP is falling".

Gina immediately noticed her patient's visibly

distended jugular veins and muffled heart sounds—Beck's triad—and knew the man's heart was failing. "His pericardium or coronary artery must have been nicked," she said aloud. "He needs his chest opened, but…"

"But what?" Ruark asked from across the room. Apparently he also had the ability to listen in on two conversations at once.

"But I'm not qualified to perform the procedure," she admitted. "He needs a surgeon. We belong upstairs, now!"

Dr Horton suddenly nudged her aside. "He won't make it as far as the elevator. Move over."

"Nice of you to join us, *Frank*," she replied caustically as she traded places with the tardy surgeon.

"Hey, I'm here now." He turned to Candy. "It'll ruin his tattoos, but get ready for a thoracotomy."

"At least he'll be alive to complain," Gina muttered.

"Only if we stop the bleeding before he goes into cardiac arrest. Scalpel."

While Frank began to work, Gina glanced at the paramedics hovering nearby. "Do we have names for these two yet?"

"I'll check." Andy slipped from the room.

Intent on assisting Frank and urging her patient

to hang on, Gina didn't notice Ruark until he stood at the foot of the bed. "How's your fellow?" she asked.

"Better than yours," he answered. "He's on his way to an operating room as we speak. They're also holding a suite open for your patient."

"And here we have it," Frank announced with distinct arrogance at discovering the problem. "His coronary artery is nicked. I'm cross-clamping the aorta and then we're out of here."

A few minutes later, Frank and the John Doe were gone. Lucy and Candy immediately began the unenviable task of dealing with the mess and, oh, what a mess it was. Instruments littered every available surface, paper wrappers and used gloves covered the blood-slickened floor.

Gina tiredly stripped off her face shield and blood-stained gown before removing her gloves, conscious of Ruark doing the same. She started to slip out of the room with the other extraneous personnel, but the sound of his voice stopped her, and everyone else, in their tracks.

"Nobody move," he commanded.

CHAPTER THREE

EVERYONE froze. Most appeared resigned, as if they were already bracing themselves for a coming storm. Determined to protect her staff, Gina immediately began her defense. "Don't blame them for not instantly following your orders. You could have been a medical student for all they knew."

Anyone with two eyes and an ounce of common sense would never believe he was a mere med student—he was far too confident and authoritative, not to mention distinguished. From the wry expression on his face, he recognized the feeble excuse for what it was.

"I'm well aware we didn't get a chance to observe the formalities, Dr Sutton," he stated as he met her gaze. "So we'll put this incident behind us. However, I am the new emergency director and I can assure every one of you I am fully qualified to handle the position."

Gina's face warmed at his rebuke. Clearly, he'd known she had sent Lucy to monitor him. Her embarrassment grew as he shared his experiences in other emergency departments and during the course of his medical relief efforts. At first, she felt guilty for having thought he was only a figurehead—a royal prince who didn't do more than lend his name in support of a cause—but how was she to have known otherwise? She hadn't even known his name before he'd waltzed in and took over. No, if anything, *he* should feel remorse for sneaking into Belmont like a burglar.

"I don't plan to change your routine overnight," he continued, "but I will be looking at your operations closely and fine-tuning those processes that need it. No matter how well a department functions, there's always room for improvement. Rest assured, I will not tolerate slipshod performances. I expect one hundred and ten percent from each of you, and intend to put forth the same effort."

Gazes met and shoulders squared as everyone seemed willing to meet his demands. It was almost surprising to see the staff co-operate so wholeheartedly this soon, but he *had* proved himself with his first case. Clearly, they were eager to impress him as well.

"What's the possibility of budgeting for more staff?" someone asked.

"If the numbers justify it, I'll do what I can to get them," he promised.

Those who had still appeared suspicious now nodded as if satisfied with Ruark's response. Slowly, skepticism and stoicism faded as he shared his vision for the department as well as a few personal facts. By the end of his impromptu meeting, not only was everyone smiling and joking with him, but they'd also learned he liked all flavors of coffee as long as they were strong, loved fresh pastries and any dessert containing apples. No doubt there would be donuts and apple pie tomorrow.

"I'm certain you'll have more questions as time goes on, but if you have a problem, my door is always open," he added in conclusion. "Meanwhile, you can return to work."

Gina accompanied him from the room while the rest of the staff headed off to deal with their respective tasks. "You had them eating out of your hand," she remarked.

His wide grin only enhanced his handsome

features. "People usually produce in accordance with the level of expectation. If they know I expect a lot, they'll deliver. If not…" He shrugged.

Determined to clear the air, she squared her shoulders and met his gaze. "For the record, I'm not sorry I'd asked Lucy to report any problems you had to me. Having never seen you in action, I'd do it again in a heartbeat."

"Under similar circumstances, I would have done the same, as would any physician who cares about his patients. I trust I've satisfied your curiosity and relieved your doubts?"

"Yes."

"Then we'll put this behind us, too."

"Why didn't you tell them you were a prince?"

"They need to see I'm a physician first and a prince second," he said simply, "otherwise they won't look past the issues of royalty and we can't form the cohesive unit we need to be."

He was obviously speaking from experience. "You told me who you are."

"Given our backgrounds, I made an exception for you."

Lucky her, she thought glumly. "I thought you prided yourself on honesty."

"I do, but do *you* want reporters swarming all

over the place, digging into your past? Believe me, it only takes one curious reporter for all of your secrets to become tomorrow's headlines. Are you ready for that, Countess?"

She gritted her teeth. "I told you before, I consider that title purely academic. I prefer to use the one I earned, and I'd appreciate it you did, too."

"I stand corrected. In any case, my personal background is irrelevant."

She scoffed. "Do you really believe that? The staff aren't blind. People will notice your bodyguards and ask questions."

"After what happened today with Bill Nevins, no one will give two extra guards a second thought. Besides, my men are professionals. They're experts at blending in. But if someone does ask questions, I'll tell them the truth. They'll find out soon enough, anyway."

His ready reply caught her off guard. "You have all the answers, don't you?" she asked waspishly, lumping in their earlier, more private discussion with this one.

"What sort of leader would I be if I didn't?" he countered. "You see, Gina, I don't like surprises."

After today, neither did she.

* * *

Ruark spent what remained of the morning observing the work flow of the department. Fortunately, no other traumas arrived, which left him free to talk individually with the staff regarding everything from scheduling to ordering supplies. He would have preferred Gina acting as his guide, but she often disappeared in other directions—"to take care of patients," she'd said.

It was only an excuse. The whiteboard indicating room assignments and diagnoses plainly showed nothing that the physician's assistant couldn't handle. However, he was willing to cut her some slack today. She clearly wanted space to digest the information he'd given her, although little did she know he'd barely scratched the surface. The rest would come this evening, when he outlined their families' proposed plan in complete detail.

When his father had first approached him and he'd read the dossier on Gina that had been compiled by the palace security team, he'd been resigned to fulfilling his obligations. After meeting her, talking to her, watching the way she handled a difficult situation, he'd become more…hopeful? about the long-term success of the scheme they had devised. Doing his duty to restore his family's honor wouldn't pose a hardship at all.

In fact, if he'd come to Belmont without any ulterior motive or agenda, if he'd only arrived as a physician who merely intended to use his medical skills until the next career move presented itself, Gina still would have captured his attention. Her elfin features, willowy frame, tawny-colored hair and special smile charmed him more than he'd imagined possible. After he'd touched her soft skin, seen the damage done by the shard of china and her blood staining his white handkerchief, he'd wanted Bill Nevins's head. For a man who prided himself on his control, his reaction amazed him.

He was almost tempted to pull rank and follow as she went about her business, to compare what he learned about her first-hand with what he'd gathered from her file, but he had to be patient. If she felt threatened and he couldn't win her over tonight, then the next few weeks wouldn't pass by pleasantly.

To his surprise and delight, he'd learned more interesting things about Gina and Belmont's emergency department from Gina's colleagues than he would have learned from her. More often than not, he heard what had fast become a familiar refrain.

"Dr Sutton takes care of that."

"Dr Sutton completes those reports."

"Dr Sutton always talks the supply department into giving us what we need."

"Dr Sutton is a stickler for continuing education," one nurse said proudly. "We're the only department in the hospital where all staff certifications are current."

At first, he'd wondered how it could be possible for one woman to accomplish so much in a given day, until he stood at the nurses' station and merely watched her go from one task to another. She might deny her heritage, but she still possessed the innate grace and regal bearing of her ancestors.

"If you're waiting until she has a free minute to talk to her, you'll be waiting a long time," Lucy warned.

He pulled his attention away from Gina and his thoughts at the sound of the nurse's voice. "Excuse me?"

"If you ever want to catch Dr Sutton, you have to do like the rest of us and just interrupt," Lucy commented. "She's in constant motion. The only time she sits down is when she's at her desk or at lunch, which she takes on a hit-and-miss basis. Sometimes just thinking about everything she does makes me tired. I don't know how she has the energy to run at full speed all day, but she does."

"I assume she stays past her shift," he said before he caught a glimpse of Gina slipping out of one exam room and into another.

"All the time," Lucy told him bluntly. "The woman doesn't have a life. She's here at 6:00 a.m. and stays until eight or nine at night, five days a week. I keep telling her she's going to burn out, but she only laughs. If you ask me, Bill Nevins took advantage of her good nature."

Ruark suspected as much.

"To be honest…" Lucy cast a sidelong glance at him "…we'd hoped that when Bill decided to retire, Gina, er, Dr Sutton would take over."

"Did you?" he replied mildly.

Lucy raised her chin. "She's done a lot for us. The staff are intensely loyal to her."

Ruark locked his gaze on hers, but she held her ground. "Is this a warning?"

"Not unless it needs to be."

He grinned at her tart tone. "Dr Sutton's place remains secure," he assured her. "Although I would appreciate it if, when Dr Sutton is relieved of some of her duties, the staff will understand it isn't because she hasn't done an excellent job. As head of Belmont's emergency department, I don't intend to follow in Bill Nevins's footsteps and shirk my own responsibilities."

"They'll understand," she promised, a smile returning to her face. "I'll see to it myself."

Certain he'd gained the head nurse's co-operation, which meant everyone else's would follow, he pointed to the schedule taped to the counter's backsplash. "Other than Gina, I rarely see the same doctor's name twice in a week."

"Because it doesn't take long for most doctors to get fed up with being overworked and under-paid, so they leave. When Gina assigns the shifts, she relies heavily on locums, friends, or previous on-staff physicians who just can't say no."

She sighed. "Then again, none of us seem to be able to say no to her. It's impossible to refuse someone who works harder and more hours than you do. She takes up a lot of the slack herself."

He thought about Frank Horton. "What about residents? Shouldn't a surgeon be available all the time?"

"Belmont only has a few residents," Lucy mentioned. "An OB-GYN who spends most of her time on the maternity floor and a neurology fellow who's usually in ICU or Rehab."

"And Frank?"

"Oh, don't let him hear you call him anything but a board-certified physician," she warned. "He's hired as a hospitalist and is assigned to our department, but he only drops by when we call him."

"He's allowed to do that?"

She shrugged. "Who's going to stop him? Gina's tried, but without having the authority she didn't get very far."

"Why didn't Nevins stand behind her?"

"As long as Frank responded in a 'timely' manner..." she emphasized the word with quotes in the air "...Bill wasn't going to force the issue." She glanced at him slyly. "If you're looking for quality improvement ideas, you should start with that one."

After dealing with cases she could have handled blindfolded, Gina had silently begged the fates to send a patient with something more complicated than shingles or an ingrown toenail. After suffering two major personal surprises today, with the arrival of both Prince Ruark and a letter from a grandmother she'd never met, she suspected the upcoming evening would have more surprises in store. Already her imagination was running rampant with possibilities of what a famous radio commentator liked to refer to as "the *rest* of the story". Rather than waste her time worrying or second-guessing what Ruark would tell her, she needed a case that required her full attention.

Fortunately for her, twenty-one-year-old Janice Myers arrived, complaining of abdominal pain.

Gina flipped through the latest lab and radiology reports. In spite of all the tests she'd run, she still couldn't pinpoint the woman's problem.

She wasn't going to give up, though.

"Your beta HCG is negative, so we can rule out an ectopic pregnancy," Gina informed Janice and her fiancé Kyle Burnham.

"I told you I wasn't pregnant," Janice said weakly as she lay on the gurney, clutching Kyle's hand in a white-knuckled grip.

"I know, but I had to check as a precaution," Gina told her kindly. "You'd be surprised how many women claim they aren't expecting and the test turns up positive."

"Then what's wrong with her, Doctor?" Kyle demanded. Tall, lanky, and wearing a mechanic's uniform, his worry was as obvious as the grease stains on his clothing. "She's been like this since last night."

"Abdominal pain, fever and your slightly elevated white blood count suggest appendicitis," Gina admitted, "although those symptoms could be due to a number of other things as well."

"Like what?"

She stuck to the more minor conditions on the list of possibilities. Suggesting Crohn's disease or cancer at this stage was premature. "Pelvic inflammatory disease," she said, thinking of how Janice only noted tenderness during her pelvic exam. "A hernia or diverticulitis, to name a few."

"What about food poisoning?" Janice asked.

"Food-borne illnesses usually manifest themselves rather abruptly. You mentioned your pain actually started two days ago and gradually grew stronger, which doesn't fit the picture."

"So what do we do now?" Kyle asked, his gaze focused on Janice. "Wait and see if the pain goes away on its own?"

Gina tucked the metal chart under one arm. "Absolutely not. I'm going to ask for a surgical consult."

"Surgery?"

Noting the horrified look the couple exchanged,

Gina explained, "Your ultrasound didn't show anything unusual, so he may decide it would be best to take a peek inside you with a laparoscope. But we'll let him decide." She patted Janice's shoulder. "Try to relax. Dr Horton should be in shortly."

She strode toward the nurses' station and plunked the chart on the counter, conscious of Ruark and Lucy at the opposite end. "Call Horton for a stat consult," she told Ruby. "Possible appendicitis in room three."

"He won't be happy," Ruby warned, her kohl-lined eyes matching her short black-out-of-a-bottle hair. "He only left a little while ago."

"I don't care if he walked out the door and has to turn around and come back—it can't be helped. My patient needs a surgery consult. If he won't come, he should send someone else."

"I'll get right on it."

"Please do."

"When you're free, Dr Sutton," Ruark interrupted as Ruby picked up the phone, "I'd like a few minutes."

She couldn't refuse, although she wanted to. At times she'd been able to pretend the events of that morning had all been a bad dream. At others the throbbing in her cheek and the occasional whiff of his expensively masculine cologne as she stepped out of a patient's cubicle reminded her otherwise. Now, with hope borne of desperation, she glanced at the whiteboard room grid.

To her regret, other than Janice's name written in room three's square, someone had wiped the board clean. "OK," she said.

If he heard her reluctance, he didn't comment. Instead, he politely followed her into his office.

She immediately noted the room's appearance as she gingerly took the chair he offered. "You've been busy."

He propped one hip on the edge of his desk. "It wasn't as bad as it looked," he admitted. "Most of the papers didn't stray too far from their folders, so it was a matter of slipping them back inside. Until I figure out the filing system, I thought it best to enlist help and Ruby obliged. According to her, you might know where these belong." He handed her a thin stack.

She quickly scanned them. "Contracts are kept in the accounting department. We certainly don't deal with real estate down here." She turned another page. "Selling equipment? We didn't sell anything…" The list of items caught her attention.

"Why, that rotten…scoundrel," she muttered under her breath.

"From your reaction, I assume you weren't aware he was selling the department's medical equipment?"

"Not at all." She shook her head before one entry caught her eye and she pointed to it. "I recognize this ophthalmology scope. We had a patient with a scratched cornea and I couldn't find it. Bill said he'd sent it out for repairs and we had to scrounge an ancient model out of storage."

"No wonder he reacted so strongly when I wouldn't give him time to clear out his desk," he mused.

"He didn't have time to hide the evidence," she agreed, handing the papers back to Ruark. "Lucky for us he threw that coffee-cup."

His gaze moved to her scratch and a muscle tensed in his jaw. "I don't happen to agree. How're you feeling?"

She gingerly touched the adhesive strip. "I'm fine. Other than an occasional throb, I hardly know it happened."

Amusement flitted into his eyes, as if he knew she wasn't being completely truthful, and she quickly changed the subject.

"Did you find anything else of interest in Bill's files?"

He folded his arms across his chest, which only emphasized the broad shoulders she found so appealing. How odd for her to be attracted to him, of all people. He was a man who represented everything her father had given up, from his responsibilities to his extended family, so how could she possibly entertain any fantasies about him?

She should get out more, she decided. She should get involved in a cause more personal than treating patients day in and day out. As rewarding as she found her job, she clearly needed an activity that met *her* needs. With nothing more than a houseplant to call her own, her hormones were plainly running amuck.

Once again, she vacillated between wanting to hear the rest of his news immediately and wanting to postpone tonight's meeting indefinitely.

"I did." His deep voice yanked her attention back where it belonged—on her job. "Surprisingly enough, underneath the mess was an organized office. After meeting my predecessor, I would never have guessed."

"First impressions can be deceiving," she said lightly.

"I also find it hard to believe he was the driving force behind the department's relatively smooth operation. But he wasn't, was he?"

Because she didn't know where he intended to go with this conversation, Gina's smile faltered. "I couldn't say," she prevaricated.

"I've been talking to our personnel," he began. "From the things they've told me of your accomplishments, I'd almost begun to wonder if you could walk on water."

She chuckled. "Trust me, I can't."

"Your people are extremely loyal to you."

The direction he was going now became clear—he was concerned about a power struggle. "Bill wasn't the easiest man to get along with. If people had a problem that I could handle, I did. And if I couldn't, I took it to him." She reflected on the times he'd blustered and bellowed, fussed and fumed, until she'd persuaded him to consider other possibilities. She definitely wouldn't miss her former boss at all. "Fortunately, I usually convinced him the situation wasn't as bad as it first appeared, or I offered more sensible options."

"Ever the diplomat."

"I did what was necessary. Otherwise we wouldn't have had a soul willing to work here longer than a week." She met his gaze. "I assume things will be different now?"

"Without question," he assured her. "I expect people to come directly to me, not hide behind you."

His command was inevitable. Although she'd wished Bill had met his responsibilities rather than leaving them for her to assume, facing the new reality was harder than she'd imagined. Whatever would she do with herself if she didn't work eighty-hour weeks?

She hid her disappointment. "Of course."

"I'm curious, though. Why didn't you let Nevins sink or swim on his own?"

"Because I got tired of dealing with crises that shouldn't have occurred, whether it was broken equipment, staffing issues, or proper procedures. I'd tried going over his head and was told to follow the proper chain of command. So, in order to treat patients, I chose to work *with* him instead of against him. I learned what made him tick."

"Which was?"

"His ego. When he complained about a certain task, I volunteered to handle it on the grounds that his time was too important to spend on trivial matters." She motioned to the papers Ruark had shown her, and smiled ruefully. "Apparently I gave him too much time."

"Did you look through his files?"

"No!" She was aghast.

"Then you shouldn't feel guilty," he said. "In the meantime, I'll alert Administration. They'll probably decide to initiate punitive action."

She nodded.

"You should also know this, Gina. I don't plan to shirk my duties."

"I'm glad to hear it."

Ruby knocked on the door. "Excuse me, Dr Sutton? Dr Horton is here and—"

Gina heard his raised voice and mentally geared herself for the inevitable confrontation. "He's not happy," she finished as she stood. "I'm coming." Without waiting for Ruark's dismissal, she joined a blustering Frank Horton at the nurses' station.

As soon as he saw her, he glared. "What is the meaning of this?" He slapped Janice Myers's chart with his knuckles.

Gina fell into her ultra-calm mode, the same tone she used to deal with recalcitrant patients as well as staff. "I asked for a surgical consult. I suspect she has appendicitis."

"I read her chart. From her symptoms, she

could have any number of conditions. Check her for food poisoning." He slid the chart across the counter where Gina caught it.

"Have you examined her yet?"

He frowned. "No. The woman doesn't need surgery. Have you thought of PID?"

"Yes, I did, but she doesn't have a history of pelvic inflammatory disease. And if PID is her problem, a laparoscopy would be helpful in the diagnosis."

"Check for parasites."

Gina held on to her temper. "I know my job," she pointed out through gritted teeth. "The test isn't necessary because her problem isn't due to intestinal parasites. She hasn't had any exposure and even if she had, the symptoms don't match."

"Surgery is already running behind schedule," he pointed out. "If she isn't better by tomorrow—"

"And if her appendix ruptures tonight?" she asked. "Or what if I'm wrong and she has a per-forated peptic ulcer, acute gangrenous cholecys-titis or some other surgical condition? Are you willing to risk the consequences of waiting another day? Because if you are, I hope you've paid your malpractice insurance premiums."

Frank hesitated. "She doesn't have appendicitis," he insisted. "She doesn't have rebound tenderness and her white count is hardly elevated."

"Fine. Do a laparoscopy and prove me wrong. I'll be happy to let you say 'I told you so'. You can post it on the bulletin board in the cafeteria too, if you'd like."

"I'm not taking her to surgery."

"Suit yourself." She moved behind the counter and grabbed the phone.

"What are you doing?" he asked.

"I'm transferring her to St Bridgit's."

"You can't do that!" he blustered.

"Watch me."

"But the paperwork! You can't justify a transfer. There'll be hell to pay," he warned.

"Yes, but I won't be the one paying. As for the paperwork? It won't be any worse than the paperwork you'll have if this woman dies."

"Don't be so melodramatic." He sounded disgusted. "She's not going to die."

"You two." Ruark's voice interrupted. "Bring this into my office. Now." He delivered his order in a tone that didn't leave room for argument.

Once inside, with the door closed, he asked, "What's the problem?"

Frank shot a triumphant look at Gina before he

began. Even as he straightened to his full height, Ruark still stood several inches over him. "Gina wants me to perform unnecessary surgery. Because I won't, she intends to transfer the patient to another hospital."

"It's not unnecessary," she countered hotly.

Ruark raised his hands. "One at a time. Dr Horton?"

Fuming inside, Gina pressed her lips together and began counting to ten.

Apparently sensing the new ED chief would be an ally, Frank ran through Janice's symptoms and test results to back his diagnosis.

"I see your dilemma," Ruark said after Frank finished.

Gina gasped, and he continued as if she hadn't made a sound. "However, it's been my experience that possible appendicitis is nothing to ignore. If Dr Sutton believes the woman needs a laparoscopy, you should honor her request."

Frank's expression changed to disbelief. "But…but—" he blustered.

"Furthermore," Ruark added, "if you can't convince Surgery to hold a suite open, perhaps your boss can arrange for one. Dr Ahmadi is the chief of surgical services, isn't he?"

"Yes, but…" Frank's face turned red.

"On second thoughts," Ruark mused, "you don't appear as if you're in the right frame of mind to operate. I'll call upstairs and locate a more *co-operative* and open-minded surgeon. After I talk to Dr Ahmadi."

Frank frowned as he squared his shoulders. "I'm a professional," he said stiffly. "I'll handle it."

"I thought you would," Ruark said smoothly. "Remember this, Dr Horton. Question Dr Sutton's judgement with such hostility again, and it will be the last time you set foot in this department."

Ruark's quiet warning took a few seconds to sink in, but eventually Frank understood. His Adam's apple bobbed as he swallowed before nodding. An instant later, he grabbed the chart out of Gina's hand and stormed away.

Gina was speechless. She'd been prepared to defend herself on behalf of Ms Myers, and now that it was completely unnecessary, she felt cheated. She should have been thrilled by the outcome, and yet…she wasn't. Ruark had defused the situation so handily, she was left with anger simmering in her veins.

"I would never demand a patient undergo un-necessary surgery," she protested.

"I know."

"I checked the woman thoroughly. She doesn't present with the classic symptoms, but my gut says—"

"Gina, I trust your instincts. Frank Horton won't give you any more trouble."

He sounded far too pleased with himself, which only added to her ire. "Apparently not," she replied stiffly.

He frowned. "I thought you'd be pleased."

"I can fight my own battles, Dr Thomas," she ground out.

"I'm sure you can, but you weren't winning this one."

She advanced. "Do you realize what you've done?"

"Saved a patient?"

"How will my colleagues ever respect my opinion if you threaten them should we ever disagree?"

"What did you want me to do? Let him yell at you as if you were a green first-year medical student?"

"No, but—"

"I stand behind my staff, and you, Gina, are mine. I don't tolerate rudeness and the sooner everyone in this hospital realizes it, the better."

It took a few seconds for his words to sink in,

and when they did, she felt foolish. "I apologize for overreacting."

"Accepted. We are a *team*," he stressed. "Problems that arise aren't yours or mine. They're *ours*. We are in this together. Remember that."

His intent gaze and the promise in his voice sent a shiver down her spine. *We are in this together. You, Gina, are mine.* She might not be an expert at reading between the lines, but she sensed undertones that he had a more proprietorial relationship in mind—a relationship that went beyond a professional employer-employee one.

In that instant, her life seemed to change before her eyes. Whether she wanted it or not, agreed to it or not, he was going to sweep her into something larger than her small world. For a woman who'd managed her life on her own, without anyone's help or interference, the idea scared her to death.

Desperate to escape until she could regain her equilibrium, she said, "I've got to go."

"Gina."

She stopped at the door. "Yes?"

"My driver will pick you up at seven."

"I'd rather drive myself."

"Not an option. Unless you'd rather we meet at your house?"

Did she want him in her home, filling it with his presence? She didn't think so. "What if I can't leave work on time?"

"Then I'll send the car here for you."

That option was worse because of the questions it would raise if anyone saw her or realized she'd left her vehicle in the parking lot. The ER staff was a sharp-eyed bunch.

Hating to give in, she had no choice. He'd won this round. "Fine," she said curtly. "I'll be ready at seven."

CHAPTER FOUR

"You have a lovely home," Gina remarked politely after Hugh had delivered her into Ruark's company later that evening.

"Thank you," he said. "May I take your jacket?"

She shrugged off the cardigan that complemented her yellow sleeveless knee-length sheath. It had taken her an hour to decide what to wear before she'd settled on this simple outfit, but after seeing Ruark, she wished she'd opted for something more elegant. He appeared informal with the sleeves of his white silk shirt rolled to his forearms and his collar and top button unfastened, but wearing his clothes in such casual abandon didn't hide the fabric's quality or the tailored fit.

"I'm surprised you found a place to live so quickly."

"Dr Lansing and his wife made the arrangements," he said. "I told them what I needed and they did the legwork."

The large foyer with its winding oak staircase and crystal chandelier definitely did not grace the houses in her moderately price neighborhood.

"It's huge. You must entertain a lot," she remarked.

"Hardly ever," he answered with a smile. "That's not to say I don't invite a few friends over, but nothing on a grand scale."

"No diplomatic events?"

"On occasion, but I don't host them at my private residence. As for the size of the house, my staff live here as well." He grinned. "Tripping over each other isn't a good idea. We all need our privacy."

As a handsome prince, much less an eligible doctor, he probably needed more privacy than most, she thought irritably.

Before she could ask what staff requirements the modern working-man prince needed, he changed the subject. "Which would you prefer first, dinner or drinks?"

"Dinner, please," she said promptly. "Lunch was a long time ago."

He grinned. "A woman after my own heart. I hope you enjoy salmon."

"I do."

"Henri will be pleased. He's been fussing over

the menu all afternoon." He seated her in the formal dining room where two places had been set at one end of a table capable of serving twelve. "I'll tell him to begin serving."

Gina studied the beautiful china before her. The crystal sparkled under the chandelier's lighting and she saw her reflection in the polished silver. Not quite the same as her chipped stoneware and stainless-steel utensils, she thought. At the same time, she realized exactly what her father had given up when he'd defied Parliament's decision—everything from having staff to see to his every need to the day-to-day tableware. Had he ever regretted his decision? She liked to think he hadn't.

Yet something he'd always told her popped into her mind.

People matter, Gina, not things.

Ruark returned a minute later and sat at the head of the table. "Did you have a comfortable ride across town?"

She'd been expecting a limo and had been pleasantly surprised her escort had arrived in a more modest vehicle instead. "Yes, although I can tell you don't need to worry about your staff spilling any secrets. I could barely drag his name out of him."

Nervous about her upcoming evening, she'd tried to draw Hugh into a normal conversation about Marestonia and, of course, Ruark, but the security guard had limited his answers to one- or two-word replies.

He smiled. "Hugh's somewhat shy, but he makes up for it in other ways. His powers of observation are phenomenal. Nothing gets by his eagle eyes."

Great, she thought irritably. He'd probably seen her flexing her Italian charm bracelet and recognized it as the nervous mannerism it was. Realizing she was toying with it now, she let go of the metal with a decided snap and dug her fingers into the napkin on her lap.

A door leading from the kitchen swung open and a portly, middle-aged balding fellow appeared with two plates in hand.

"Gina, this is Henri. Henri, Dr Sutton."

"Pleased to meet you, *mademoiselle*." Henri set a plate of spinach salad before her. "The prince has spoken of you often."

She raised an eyebrow at Ruark before turning to smile at his chef. "Good things, I hope," she answered lightly.

"Oh, my, yes. All good things. Enjoy your

meal." After placing Ruark's salad in front of him, he bowed, then disappeared.

"Henri's been with me for several years," Ruark offered. "He's quite temperamental when it comes to food."

"Oh?" She took a bite and nearly groaned with delight. The dressing had definitely not come out of a bottle.

"He's a stickler for timing. If anyone is five minutes late, he complains about dinner being ruined."

"You and your staff eat together?"

"Are you shocked?"

"A little," she admitted. "I didn't think a prince would associate with hired help. Protocol and all that."

"There are a few lines I don't cross, but dinner isn't one of them. You see, I hate to eat alone."

Gina did, too. Which was why she often stayed at the hospital and ate her evening meal at the cafeteria. Even if she sat by herself, hearing bits and pieces of conversations at other tables was better than having the television for company.

Maybe she should get a dog, although it wouldn't be fair for the poor creature to be alone all day.

"Perhaps you'll agree to join our group some time," he added.

"Perhaps," she answered, unwilling to commit herself although the idea intrigued her.

While Henri's grilled salmon, herb-roasted potatoes and glazed baby carrots gave her taste buds a real treat, Ruark entertained her with humorous stories from his previous jobs. Halfway through the meal, she became so focused on her companion and so caught up in their conversation, that she forgot the purpose behind her visit and began enjoying herself. Reality, however, set in after Ruark offered to serve coffee and dessert in his study. She hadn't made a purely social call.

"I'd like to thank you for coming tonight so we can discuss the problem before us," he said as he guided her into a room filled with a large oak desk, several Queen Anne chairs and a sofa covered in matching maroon and gold brocade, and built-in bookcases filled with tomes of all shapes and sizes.

She sank into a chair, noting he'd taken the one opposite. "I'm not convinced this is my problem."

"Poor choice of words. The *situation* before us."

"Why don't you cut to the bottom line and save us both some time?" she suggested.

"I'd rather start at the beginning. Just to be sure you understand what happened and why it affects current events."

"Suit yourself, but I'm not promising anything," she warned.

"Understood." He took a deep breath. "As you may know, in Avelogne, as in Marestonia, the government approves the marriages of the royal family as a formality. Unfortunately, when your father requested permission to marry your mother, Parliament denied his petition."

"Which was why he relinquished his claim to the throne and came to America," she finished. "Yes, I've heard the story of how a group of small-minded men in power didn't feel my mother had the right..." she drew imaginary quotation marks in the air "...'connections'. I never understood what the right connections would have been, other than she was a commoner instead of a royal."

"Our governments are more progressive in their beliefs than to get hung up on the royalty-versus-commoner issue," he pointed out somewhat defensively. "However, their decision was based on what appeared to be irrefutable evidence indicating that the royal family could be placed in a compromising position if Prince Arthur and Lizbet VanHorn married."

Her father had never mentioned any so-called evidence. "And this information was…?"

He hesitated, and Gina pressed on. "There can't be any secrets, Ruark. I have to know *everything*, good or bad."

Ruark cleared his throat. "Lizbet's father worked for a man who dealt in illegal activities, so there were suspicions of his involvement."

Illegal activities? Her dear, sweet grandpapa Jorge had been a criminal? He'd died when she'd been six—about five years before her mother's accident—but she couldn't believe the man who'd smelt of peppermints and tobacco and taken her to the park with a bag of day-old bread to feed the pigeons had been a part of the criminal element. Had her whole life, her family's seemingly normal life, all been a lie?

"Those activities were?" She raised an eyebrow.

"Drugs, prostitution, and anything else you can think of. Because of that association, your parents conducted their romance in secret. Your mother taught music at the primary level, lived a quiet, sedate life and was well liked, so Arthur believed his petition to marry her would be granted. After all, she couldn't be blamed or held accountable for her father's or his employer's actions.

"Unfortunately, as I've already told you, my aunt Margret had developed feelings for Arthur and was crushed when he didn't return her affections. Consequently, she, shall we say, *embellished* certain facts and arranged for the committee to receive information that called Lizbet's character into question."

"Embellished? Let's not sugar-coat this, Ruark. In other words, she *lied*."

He sighed. "Whatever term you wish to use, there was enough truth in the story to make the evidence appear irrefutable. That, coupled with a doubt here, a question there, and the members of the committee subsequently hesitated to give their approval."

"So that's why they denied his request." For the first time in her life she'd heard specific details, and her heart ached for her parents.

"Prince Arthur refused to let the government dictate his personal life so, against the Queen's wishes, he relinquished any future claims to the throne. His decision rocked the country but, being a second son, he was able to smooth over the issue with reminders that his chances of assuming the position of King were minimal at best. Because he publicly insisted how much he loved his future wife."

"He did," she insisted.

"No one is denying that. However, the people of Avelogne were incensed with Marestonia, accusing them of dishonesty and all manner of evil plots. In order to defuse the volatile situation, Arthur played on the people's romantic sympathies. He worked tirelessly for the two countries to maintain diplomatic ties, citing that this was a private matter and not a political one. Eventually, tempers softened as his appearances with your mother proved his sincerity, so everyone bowed to the inevitable and reluctantly accepted his decision. He married Lizbet and they moved to America, where you were born."

The story brought tears to Gina's eyes, but she blinked them away. "Didn't they try and prove Mother's innocence, not to mention my grandfather's?"

"The circumstantial evidence was too strong. And, I'm sorry to say, the royal family wanted the incident to die down as quickly as possible." He met her gaze. "I don't believe your grandmother expected Arthur to act as he did, but once he set the wheels in motion, she had to uphold the laws governing succession."

"And Margret? What happened to her?"

"She never married."

Gina swallowed the lump in her throat. "How did you learn the truth? If no one had been able to ferret out the facts at the time, how could anyone thirty years later?"

"Your uncle and my father quietly investigated from the beginning, but they kept running into dead ends. Witnesses disappeared, documents vanished, memories failed, until finally Arthur insisted they accept what they couldn't change. A few years ago Margret was diagnosed with a virulent form of brain cancer. In her diary, which we found shortly after her death, she admitted to her role in the scandal."

"Was she honest?"

"As honest as anyone would be when faced with their own mortality," Ruark replied. "We didn't have reason to doubt her account as she supplied all the information we needed. Names, dates, places."

"I see."

"It seemed pointless to act. Arthur and Lizbet had both died by then, too. Dredging up the old memories seemed counterproductive, although the few members of the committee who still sat in Parliament quietly resigned their positions."

"Bully for them."

"For the record," he continued, "your grand-mother, the Queen Mother, regrets the events leading to your father's decision to leave Avelogne. She'd always hoped for a reconciliation, and his death upset her greatly. They would be grateful if you would agree to visit them some day soon."

"You can thank them for the invitation, but it isn't likely," she said politely. "It's too difficult to get away from the hospital."

Her excuse was flimsy, especially as the man who could arrange it in a heartbeat sat a few feet away, but he didn't argue.

"Regardless of the role Prince Arthur's family played in these events," he continued, "the bulk of the blame falls on the house of Marestonia."

Gina tried to tie the ends together, but couldn't. "Assigning blame isn't necessary," she mused aloud. "I appreciate finally knowing the truth, but it doesn't change what happened. Honestly? I don't see why this should be causing a problem now if the appropriate people knew the truth several years ago."

"Margret's diary recently fell into the wrong hands," he admitted, "and the information went public. The hostilities resurfaced because to the people of Avelogne this was one more in a long line of what they considered as poor decisions made by the ruling class."

"None of this makes sense," she protested. "If you're unhappy with your officials, you don't cause problems for other countries."

"You do if you feel the government has given those other countries, Marestonia in particular, favored status. You see, in trying to increase imports and exports, they granted special tax dispensations to Marestonian citizens who opened businesses or conducted trade in Avelogne. Now, with this news coming out, it's the proverbial last straw and they want their pound of flesh."

"Which is why they're pressuring Parliament to vote on severing economic ties to Marestonia," she finished, finally understanding the dynamics.

"Yes. I've already explained the repercussions to both countries should that happen."

"Then offer an official apology. Take away the tax exemptions."

"Both Avelogne and Marestonia have prided themselves on their openness and honesty with each other. Many feel an apology isn't enough. As for the tax, I believe your Parliament plans to address the issue."

"Your family could build a new hospital or a school in my father's honor. That should make everyone happy."

"Excuse me, Your Highness." Hugh stepped into the room. "You must see this latest news report."

While Ruark opened the oak cabinet which hid the large-screen TV, Hugh immediately retrieved the remote and clicked on the set.

A picture flashed to a street where hundreds of people lined the sidewalks in front of a large building that Gina recognized as Avelogne's Parliament. Some carried signs, others chanted or waved angry fists at police who stood nearby in full riot gear.

A female reporter's voice explained the scene.

"As you can see," the nameless woman began, "people have come to the seat of government in response to a grass-roots effort to force Parliament into correcting what is perceived as a careless decision some thirty years ago involving Prince Arthur and his bride-to-be, Lizbet VanHorn. The mood is tense as most people here demand the authorities sever diplomatic ties with Marestonia. A number of people have already been arrested for inciting the crowd and it's obvious neither the government nor the royal family has a ready solution to this growing discontent.

"Businesses owned by Marestonians are being boycotted and many of them report they cannot keep their doors open or will be forced to lay off their employees if this continues. A number have reported increased amounts of vandalism ranging from broken windows to obscene graffiti."

The camera panned to one area where fisticuffs had broken out between several young men and police, then switched to show several others breaking car windows with rocks and tire irons. One view zoomed in on a child crying in his mother's arms after the family had been evicted from their apartment.

"As you can see," the announcer continued, "we have a volatile situation and if it escalates, Parliament has already threatened to set curfews and deploy national troops to maintain order."

Gina hardly noticed when Ruark clicked off the television. The screen had gone dark, but she was still taking in what she had seen and heard. "I thought you were exaggerating," she admitted, reeling from what she'd seen. "But you weren't, were you?"

He shook his head, then sat down. "No."

She faced him. "According to the reporter, no one in authority has a solution. What do you think I can do?"

"Diplomacy doesn't seem to be having an effect. The experts believe a more 'personal' solution between our families is required."

"We're already working with each other," she reminded him.

The corners of his mouth turned up slightly. "It's a start, but they're hoping to tie the two royal houses together."

"How would you tie two royal houses…?" Her voice died as she realized exactly the sort of "personal" relationship he wanted. "You can't possibly be thinking of…"

He finished her sentence. "Marriage."

Marriage.

The word echoed in her head.

Marriage.

To a man she'd only met earlier in the day.

After years of working in the ER, she'd always considered herself unshockable, but that one word definitely shifted the ground underneath her. "We're supposed to get married?" she managed to croak.

He leaned forward and rested his elbows on his knees. "Yes."

Her heart pounded and an urge to escape swept over her. "This is a joke, right?"

"Not at all."

Her mind raced with possibilities. "You mean to tell me the diplomats of two countries can't dream up a better solution than to ask two strangers to marry?"

"We considered other options, but lawsuits, financial settlements, and economic sanctions are cold comfort to a person's pride. Those solutions would also cause undue hardship on both countries. I've seen too many hungry children in my relief work. I don't have a desire to see the same sad faces and malnourished bodies at home."

"Of course I don't want anyone to lose his job or go hungry," she snapped. "What kind of person do you think I am?"

"The sort who will do the right thing."

The enormity of the situation struck her and she rubbed the back of her neck. "This day can*not* be happening," she muttered. "It can't. First Bill, and now this. It's all a dream."

"I assure you it isn't," Ruark said.

She met his gaze. "The idea of using marriage as a diplomatic measure is so *medieval*!"

"Medieval or not, the practice isn't unheard of. Wars have been started over the very issue standing between Avelogne and Marestonia."

"Not in this day and age."

He raised an eyebrow. "Really? Tell that to all the countries who believe another has slighted them for whatever reason."

"Oh, great. You're going to hold me responsible for starting a war?"

"Matters won't go to that extreme, but strained relations won't do either country any good."

She shook her head. "No, but I can't believe a sane person actually proposed this as a solution or that two entire families gave it merit."

"I can assure you the Queen Mother of Avelogne is perfectly sane. As for the idea having merit, desperate times call for desperate measures."

Desperate times, desperate measures. She understood the concept.

"Look," she began, "I'm flattered you think I can help. I'm flattered that you, as a prince, would seriously consider marrying me sight unseen, but no one will believe we're sincere. Things are moving much too fast to be believable, unless you're thinking of a platonic marriage which we'll annul in a year or so." She raised an eyebrow.

"No annulment. No platonic marriage. This is for real."

So much for that idea. "Marriage is a big step to a couple who know each other, much less between two people who don't. The fact we're complete strangers may be a small, insignificant detail to you, but it isn't to me and I doubt if it is to everyone else. The people of both countries will see it as a ploy to manipulate them and they'll be right."

"Not if we convince everyone otherwise."

"I'm a physician, not an actress," she reminded him.

"Exactly." He sounded pleased. "No one will question a romantic relationship between two people who share the same career and work in the same facility."

The pieces fell into place—delivering the letter from her grandmother had only been a small part of the overall scheme. "You'd planned this all along, didn't you?"

His gaze locked on hers. "Of course. A marriage with the two of us on opposite sides of the country would draw suspicion."

"No one can pack up and move overnight. Job openings don't appear because you want them either."

"They don't," he agreed. "I began making inquiries several months ago."

Several months ago? "Don't tell me you had Bill Nevins fired so you could take his place." She didn't want to think of the sort of power Ruark might hold if he'd accomplished that feat.

"According to what I was told, Bill's management style had concerned Administration for some time. They'd been biding their time and quietly looking for a replacement so when I approached them about a position here, they were ready to act. It was the perfect opportunity for all of us. Except Nevins, of course."

Now she understood how a game piece token felt as the player moved it along according to the roll of the dice. Arranging the events that had brought the two of them to this point must have been as precisely orchestrated as a military campaign.

"Aren't you going out on a limb?" she asked, certain she'd found an ace up her sleeve. "What if I walk out that door and don't come back? You'll be stuck here, I'll be gone, and your grand scheme will fall apart."

"You won't leave."

She snorted at his confidence. "Don't be too sure."

"Oh, I'm sure, Gina." His dark gaze grew more intent and she sensed he would be a formidable opponent. "You see, you need this job because you're as proud as your father. As a matter of principle, he didn't use the funds the royal family provided when he left Avelogne and you haven't either, even though it would have made it completely unnecessary to borrow money to finance medical school. In fact, you and your father have already planned to leave the money to charity should anything happen to you. Half to an orphanage in Avelogne and the other half to—"

She was amazed by his unerring accuracy. "How do you know that?"

"You would be surprised what I know, but I can safely say you won't run away." He ticked off his points on his fingers. "One, you need a job, so you either must keep this one or find another. Two, you won't find another without a reference and guess who currently is responsible for writing one on your behalf?

"Three," he continued, "your contract states you must give ninety days' written notice. If you fail to honor those terms, we're back to reason number two. So, your argument about marrying a stranger is inconsequential because, one way or another, we'll be together for the next three months. We won't be strangers for long."

Darn the man, he was right!

"And if I refuse your gracious proposal?"

He raised one eyebrow. "I'm known to be quite persuasive."

She didn't doubt that a bit. Having met him less than twelve hours ago, she'd already seen evidence of his dogged determination to succeed at any cost. Plus, she was on *his* turf, without any form of transportation other than her own two feet, which meant he could hold her here for hours. Clearly, the odds of standing her ground weren't in her favor.

"Why are you accepting arrangements made without your consent?" she wanted to know. "It isn't as if you're the heir apparent. If you can choose your own career, you can surely choose your own wife."

As she spoke, she wondered what sort of woman he would have married if given the choice. Irrationally, the thought that she might not have attracted his attention under normal circumstances pricked her self-esteem.

"I can," he assured her. "For me, though, this is a matter of family honor and duty."

How could she argue with something so intangible, yet so powerful? "Just what every woman wants to hear," she said dryly. "A proposal offered out of duty."

He raised an eyebrow. "Would you rather I had pursued you for several weeks, professed enduring love and then rushed you to the altar? Eventually, you would have learned the truth and hated me for my dishonesty, which wouldn't have boded well for any marriage."

Once again, he was right, and she found his uncanny perception as irritating as his impersonal proposal. "What if I already *have* a fiancé?" she blustered.

CHAPTER FIVE

RUARK smiled, as if he knew she was grasping for an excuse. "You don't. You haven't dated anyone seriously for a number of months."

At least he hadn't pointed out her last date had been for the previous year's hospital Christmas party. Even so, he didn't need to sound so pleased with himself for pointing it out.

"I know more about you, Gina," he continued, "than you think I do."

What a scary thought. "There has to be an alternative," she said, desperately trying to think of one and failing miserably.

"If you think of one that our diplomats and scholars have overlooked, I'm willing to listen."

She had nothing, at least at the moment. "Look," she began, "for your plan to work, you're assuming we're compatible. What if we're not?"

"What if we are?" he countered. "We'll never know if we don't put in an effort."

She argued her case from another angle. "Why don't you issue a press release announcing that you proposed but I refused? You can claim you tried to do the right thing, but I didn't co-operate."

"Do you think my countrymen will be satisfied once they hear you've rejected their prince without cause, after knowing him less than twenty-four hours? They'll take it as a personal insult."

"Better to feel insulted than manipulated," she pointed out. "Knowing you proposed less than a day after meeting me isn't going to promote good public relations either. Neither is inventing a story to fool millions of people. Two wrongs don't make a right and being anything less than perfectly honest is a prescription for disaster."

"Stretching the truth goes against the grain with me, too," he admitted, "but we simply state the barest of facts and allow the press to draw their own conclusions. As luck would have it, we both attended the emergency medicine conference in Los Angeles six months ago. Registration records from both the conference and the hotel will prove it to anyone who questions us. People will logically believe we met and struck up a long-distance romance that led to me relocating to Belmont."

"You were at the conference?" Granted, there

had been thousands in attendance, but how could she have missed him?

"All five days," he assured her.

This whole situation was spiraling more and more out of control. "Am I the only one who sees the inherent failure in this so-called *plan*?"

"We won't allow it to fail. It's the best solution, as far as I can see."

The man had to be blind, she thought, exasperated by his calm acceptance of the situation. "I don't know the first thing about being a princess. And in case you haven't noticed, things like this *just aren't done these days*!"

"Being a princess won't be any different than being a countess. You'll wake up every morning, go to work, and come home at night to your family."

Family. The term implied a husband, children, and everything associated with them—piano recitals, ball games, school events. She'd wished for relatives after her mother had died in a car accident and she'd had no one left except her father, but the demands of medical school and her career had pushed those dreams to the back of her mind. Realizing they could now be within reach, that they now fell in the realm of probability rather than possibility, was almost more than she dared to imagine. More importantly, the prospect of Ruark playing a prominent role in that scenario caused her toes to curl.

Yet, she'd learned a few lessons over the years. Few situations were as simple as they initially appeared.

"You've clearly forgotten how I was raised. My royal background was simply historical information, like having an ancestor who served in the First World War. It didn't factor into who I am today."

"Perhaps not entirely," he agreed. "We chose medicine as our profession and I doubt if either of us will give it up, so the major part of our lives won't change. Oh, we may have to appear at a diplomatic event every now and then but, I can assure you, those instances are rare. Probably a few times a year."

He was entirely too agreeable to a scenario that could end in a lifetime of disaster. She narrowed her gaze. "What's in this for you? Is someone giving you the keys to the national treasury, or what?"

His eyes reflected his gentle smile. "I had my doubts, too," he admitted, "but when I considered the repercussions if I refused to put the needs of my people before my own, my worries seemed insignificant in comparison."

While she hadn't expected him to swear undying love after a few hours and wouldn't have believed him if he had, she would like to think she was more than another obligation he had to fulfill. And yet it was silly to wish for that—they'd only met ten hours ago.

"I realize this idea is difficult to consider, much less accept," he said kindly. "But your father worked tirelessly to prevent what you saw from happening thirty years ago. Are you willing to let it happen today, when you have the power to prevent it?"

People matter, Gina, not things.

Knowing how much her father had loved Avelogne, she found herself actually giving Ruark's proposal serious thought…

"I don't want my father's efforts to have been in vain," she admitted, "but marriage should be based on more than politics, especially if it's supposed to endure through good times as well as bad."

"Ours will be," he assured her. "We have enough common interests to form a foundation for a satisfying life together."

Common interests. A satisfying life. It sounded

as exciting as a bland diet. "When have you and your cronies planned this happy event, provided I agree, of course?"

"As soon as it can be arranged."

"As soon as…?" She didn't attempt to hide her shock. Marrying Ruark at some distant point in the future was a difficult enough concept to wrap her head around, but doing so as soon as possible? A shiver went down her spine, but she couldn't decide if fear or some twisted sense of anticipation caused her reaction.

"Why the rush? Why not, say, six months?" Surely in that length of time the crisis would resolve itself or she would find a another solution.

"Six months? Impossible. Time is of the essence. Discontent grows with every day we delay."

She'd seen the newscast, so she couldn't argue his point. "Yes, but rushing to the altar will only raise more questions." She eyed him closely. "I do hope you aren't going to hint a royal baby's involved."

He grinned. "That's an idea no one's considered. I'm sure we'll make beautiful babies."

A mental picture of a long, lean masculine form tangled in sheets, his whisker-rough face relaxed in sleep as he spooned his body against hers created a sudden and unsettling ache in her core.

She rubbed her forehead with an unsteady hand to dispel the image, and it instantly changed. A boy with Ruark's dark hair and impish smile appeared, followed by a little girl who resembled Gina in her childhood photos. They were definitely beautiful children, but this wasn't the time to think about offspring.

She drew a cleansing breath as she blinked away the vision. "Whether we will or won't isn't the issue," she stated firmly. "The point is, don't you dare suggest I'm pregnant because I can guarantee your story will backfire."

He raised one eyebrow. "Will it?"

Something in his eyes suggested that he wouldn't mind making a baby a reality. As for her, the notion of sharing a bed, feeling his intimate touch on her bare skin, was enough to send another wave of heat coursing through her. Marrying a man out of duty—a man she'd just met—wasn't supposed to cause such an intense reaction, was it?

She struggled to rein in her thoughts. "We aren't going to muddy the waters any more than they already are," she ordered, hoping he hadn't noticed how breathless she sounded.

He paused. "Perhaps it's for the best," he

mused, "but, as I said before, time is our enemy. Parliament will vote at the end of October to sever diplomatic ties, so the sooner we act, the better."

"Maybe everyone will be satisfied with an engagement announcement," she suggested hopefully.

He shook his head. "If we don't follow through with a wedding, the whole plan will seem contrived and we'll have worse problems. There's truly no sense in prolonging the inevitable."

Reluctantly, she saw his point. Better to rip off the adhesive bandage rather than tear it off in tiny, painful increments. "Tell me how this is going to work," she said tiredly, hoping he hadn't noticed how she'd slipped and used the present tense.

"I'll arrange for a civil ceremony as soon as possible. Once our union is official, my father will announce our marriage and we'll begin our life as a couple."

A civil ceremony. Not quite the wedding she'd imagined but, then, she'd never dreamed about marrying a man she didn't love in a business arrangement.

"How do you explain why we're not having an official state wedding?"

"You want to be married in the US because it's been your home," he said simply. "With your

father deceased, you preferred a private gather-
ing with only your closest friends. No one will
question your decision."

"Other than we're rushing into this."

"Rushing only adds to the romanticism," he
assured her. "Especially if we hint at our impa-
tience to be together after I moved to Belmont."

He'd thought of everything, which irritated her.
"Am I allowed to choose my own dress, or have
you organized that, too?"

He went on as if he hadn't noticed the sarcasm
in her voice.

"After the ceremony, we act as any married
couple. A few photos and a couple of carefully
screened interviews should convince everyone
in Marestonia and Avelogne to put the past
behind them."

"And if we fight like cats and dogs?"

His now-familiar half-smile appeared. "We
won't."

"How can you be so sure?"

"Gut feeling."

"And if you're wrong?"

"I'm not."

"But if you are?" she persisted.

He leaned forward. "We're both adults and

know what's at stake. We have to make this work, Gina. We *can* make it work."

He sounded so certain, but was he trying to convince himself or her?

She couldn't deny her physical attraction to him, but she'd always imagined experiencing a grand passion. Considering how her father had sacrificed everything to marry the woman he'd loved, how could she do any less, no matter how handsome or charming the man was? And yet how could she ignore the repercussions if she didn't do something to calm the troubled waters?

"You may not find me as distasteful as you imagine."

He'd spoken lightly, but she sensed his hurt. He'd argued his case in such coolly logical terms that she'd forgotten her lack of co-operation was as much a rejection of him as it was for the plan he'd presented.

Her face warmed and she tried to minimize the damage. "I'm sorry, Ruark. My objections aren't directed toward you personally. I'd always imagined I'd have a marriage like my parents', not one borne out of convenience or duty. And certainly not one that was forced upon me to solve a national crisis."

He nodded, as if he understood. "It does take a bit of time to grow accustomed to the idea."

She met his gaze. "How long did it take *you* to become a willing participant in this…this plan?"

He shrugged. "You forget I was raised to place my country's needs before my own. If one looks at the big picture, there are far worse things I could do than marry a beautiful woman who shares my passion for medicine."

She wondered if he was simply spouting flattery to get on her good side, but there probably *were* worse things she could have been asked to do. However, at the moment she couldn't think of what could be worse than marrying a man she'd just met, regardless of how attractive he was.

"And if this grand scheme doesn't work?" she asked. "If people don't care about our marriage?"

"They will," he assured her. "Trust me." He paused. "Are you willing to marry me, Gina?"

Ruark's question hung in the air. Was she willing?

Hardly, she thought. Unfortunately, as Gina glanced at the now-darkened television screen, the newscast and Ruark's predictions haunted her. As much as she hated to be a pawn, she *was* her father's daughter, which meant she had to uphold her father's reputation. How well would the people of his homeland remember him if she, as his daughter, ignored their problems?

She may not have been raised under the same strict code of duty and honor that Ruark had been, but she, too, had learned similar lessons from her father. More importantly, she carried enough royal blood in her veins to know she couldn't besmirch Arthur Sutton's memory or do anything that would reflect poorly on her beloved papa. Holding out for a so-called "grand passion" that might never occur was too high a price to pay.

"I'll go along with the plan," she reluctantly agreed, "but I'm concerned about one thing." She met his gaze with steel in her own.

"Which is?"

"What if you meet someone else? Someone you fall in love with? What then?"

"I won't."

She eyed him with skepticism. "You don't know that."

"I'm thirty-five years old, Gina. I've dated my share of women and been involved in a number of relationships. Falling in love is an overrated concept, especially when one considers the problems Margret's so-called love for your father has created," he added dryly. "Far better for both parties to build a relationship on respect and mutual interests rather than on something as changeable as emotions."

Thinking of her parents' love for each other, the lengths they had gone to just to be together, she disagreed. "You have a rather cynical view."

He shrugged. "The best one can hope for is congenial companionship. I believe we can find it in the course of carrying out our duty."

He'd used that word again. Duty. Never had such a tiny word carried such a heavy burden, but she'd made a promise. As she studied her future husband, a variety of emotions swirled around her. Marriage to a handsome man who wore sex appeal like a well-fitting garment was both exciting and nerve-racking. For a woman who'd placed the prospect at some distant point in the future, knowing that the future was *now* was quite scary, too.

"Let's hope so," she agreed. "But this marriage…" She paused. "You truly want it to be real."

He nodded. "In every sense."

Once again, her hand trembled. "Yes, but—"

"We won't be convincing if it isn't," he said gently.

"I know, but making…" Knowing his views on the subject, she bit off the word "love" and corrected herself. "Having sex with a stranger, much less my boss, is going to be difficult."

"Not if you think of me as your husband first."

Husband. Her mouth suddenly went dry at the thought.

"But," he continued, nodding as if he understood her dilemma, "I understand your concerns so I'll give you time to adjust."

"How much?"

He met her gaze and the heat she saw in those depths reminded her of a lion she'd seen on television eyeing a tasty doe. "We'll play it by ear," he finally said.

While she would have preferred a specific date, knowing he would give her the luxury of getting to know each other first helped ease her mind about their quasi-business arrangement. "OK."

"Good. I'll set the wheels in motion." He rose then, as if he'd sensed her inner turmoil, stopped in front of her chair, pulled her into his embrace and tucked her head underneath his chin. "This will work out, you'll see."

"I'm not as sold on the idea as you are," she said wryly as she held herself stiffly against him.

"I have enough confidence for both of us," he said before he tipped her chin up to kiss her.

The pressure of his mouth was gentle, his hold on her loose enough that she could break free if she wanted to, but that made all the difference. Instead of feeling trapped, she felt reassured, as if he'd transferred his faith to her through that small but intimate contact. Earlier in the day her instincts had told her she could trust him as a physician. Now her trust had somehow expanded to include the entire man.

As she inhaled his scent and found it utterly delightful, she relaxed against him, conscious of how this simple kiss had sealed their agreement in a way that mere words or a handshake could never have accomplished.

Slowly, almost reluctantly, he raised his head, and she pulled away as the special moment passed. Unsure of what to say or do next, she simply met his gaze and offered a small smile, which he returned.

"Your father would be proud of you," he said simply.

She'd like to think so, but she also knew how strongly he adhered to his principles. "Would he? I'm not so sure he'd approve of a pretend romance. After all, we're not being completely honest, are we?"

"We're being honest enough. As for a romance, few will concern themselves with how it begins. Only with how it ends."

Ruark strolled into Belmont's ER the next morning with a smile on his face and a spring in his step. Last night had gone better than he'd initially hoped. In fact, he suspected the newscast had done more to persuade her than anything he'd said. No matter how it had happened, Gina had finally agreed, and that was all that mattered.

It wasn't until he began the detailed tour of what would soon become her home that he realized the enormity of his situation.

He was getting married.

Acquiring Gina as his wife wasn't a mere theory or a step-by-step plan any longer. Promises had been exchanged and he felt more committed now than he had when he'd first agreed to perform his duty.

He would have a spouse and, eventually, children to call his own.

The additional responsibility bore down on him, but he wasn't afraid or nervous. As he'd kissed her, the most delightful hungry sensation had swept over him. Her feminine scent and the way she had felt in his arms had made it difficult to maintain his control. Pouncing on her while they had been sealing their bargain would have been completely inappropriate, but he would be patient. Their strong physical attraction seemed to confirm that they would enjoy the same companionship his parents did.

In spite of his parents' urging over the years, he hadn't met anyone he'd wanted to marry or whom he'd considered a potential bride until Gina. But with her, he'd felt an indefinable "click" between them, as if fate had already decreed they belonged together. That feeling was more important than the nebulous emotion of love that so many searched for and rarely found.

Her worries about him falling in love with someone after they were married were completely groundless. He'd been with plenty of women who'd professed to love him, then had left when their eyes had landed on someone else. Friendship, coupled with a significant dose of lust, was love enough for him and certainly didn't make one as vulnerable. He wasn't looking for, or expecting, more than that and he believed he'd made his feelings clear. He didn't want her to harbor any false expectations.

As for Gina's expectations, she'd been re-markably close-mouthed during their tour of his home. He'd half expected her to balk and protest at sharing his bedroom, but she hadn't. Her face had paled, but she hadn't shown any other reaction. Instead, she'd tentatively asked if she could move her mother's oak quilt stand into a corner.

It had been the first—and only—request she'd made. By then he would have agreed to anything just to see a smile.

Something inside him cautioned him on the importance of smoothing her transition into her new life. If not, they'd never develop the sort of amicable relationship he wanted, much less the sort necessary for their plan to work.

Yet he had other reasons for wanting to minimize the stress of a quick wedding. She'd looked lost, as if everything she'd ever known or believed in had been ripped out from under her and her forlorn expression had tugged at his gut.

When she found her footing again, he wanted to figure prominently in the picture, to be the rock she leaned on, just as his friends' wives leaned on their husbands. It was the only way their relationship would work.

Of course, their mutual interest in medicine was a plus, and the physical attraction that arced between them practically guaranteed a successful marriage. He'd been resigned to performing his duty, but now he was actually looking forward to it.

In fact, he was quite glad the political analysts didn't believe a mere engagement would solve Marestonia and Avelogne's problems. Nothing but a wedding ring on her finger would prove the two families had worked through their differences, and he was more than happy to oblige.

While he might be eager to fulfill his royal obligations, Gina clearly was not. Working together would present ample opportunity to develop a relationship that would calm her fears, starting now….

He rounded the corner and saw her standing with several staff members at the nurses' station, wearing a freshly starched lab coat over a deep purple scrub suit. Her shoulder-length hair gleamed under the fluorescent lights and reminded him of the young lioness he'd seen at the grand opening of the Marestonia National

Zoo. Just seeing her made him forget his briefcase full of papers to review and the rainy-day forecast.

"Good morning," he said casually as he approached, trying to tone down his enthusiasm at seeing her again.

Gina's face turned a becoming shade of pink. "Good morning," she mumbled warily.

Determined to set her at ease, he turned on his professional demeanor.

"Anything interesting?" he asked as he glanced at the board. Four rooms were occupied, which wasn't unusual for a morning. After translating the shorthand, the diagnoses included emphysema, an orthopedic consult, a diabetic, and the one thing that sent people running to the ED— chest pain.

"Um, yeah, the orthopedic consult."

"Unusual sports injury?"

"In a manner of speaking. A lady fell off her high heels. Poor thing."

"What happened?"

"She'd overslept this morning and was running out to her car when her heel caught in a sidewalk crack. She started to fall, and twisted her knee in the hope she'd save her panty hose."

"No kidding?"

"Hey, snagging one's last pair of panty hose is serious business. Anyway, she landed wrong and heard her knee pop."

"Torn ACL?" he asked, using the abbreviation for the anterior cruciate ligament.

"I'd say so, but I'm waiting for Tribble, the orthopedic surgeon, to drop by. If it is her ACL, she's looking at surgery and lots of physical therapy. In the meantime, she's icing her knee and swearing off high heels." She smiled ruefully. "The price we pay for fashion."

"You have to admit, high heels are rather sexy."

"Really? You think so?" She sounded interested in his opinion.

"Trust me, they are." He raised his briefcase as he dropped his teasing tone. "About our ceremony…"

"What about it?" she asked hurriedly, taking one step toward his office in an obvious attempt to hold their conversation in more private surroundings.

Sensing Lucy's and the ward clerk's interest, he didn't budge. "It's tomorrow night, eight o'clock. In the chapel upstairs."

Her eyes widened. "How…? When…did you arrange that?"

"'Where there's a will, there's a way'." He

cheerfully quoted the cliché. "Actually, I've been busy this morning."

In truth, he'd hardly slept at all last night. After he'd taken Gina home, he'd dialed his father's private extension to break the news to his ecstatic parents. Not only did Gina's acceptance signal the beginning of the end to their current problems, but their youngest son, who'd fiercely vowed to remain single, was getting married after all.

No doubt the palace staff had been as busy as his own after their conversation had ended.

"What ceremony?" Lucy asked, curiosity oozing out of her.

Ruark slid one arm around Gina's waist and hugged her close. "We're getting married and everyone's invited."

CHAPTER SIX

WE'RE getting married....

Ruark's announcement couldn't have been more shocking or exciting to the ER staff than a ten-million-dollar lottery win. Staff members suddenly appeared from out of nowhere and fired question after question until her head spun.

"How did you two meet? We want details," someone cried out.

"How long have you planned this?"

"Are you going on a honeymoon?"

Gina had never run from problems before, but certainly wanted to now. Ruark had created this sideshow and he could deal with it, she thought unreasonably, yet she knew she belonged at his side. Leaving him to fend questions by himself would cause people to speculate and draw the wrong conclusions, which would cause the plan to fall apart.

So she allowed him to anchor her to his hip and

tried to look like an excited soon-to-be bride. It was difficult at first, but being surrounded by his masculine scent, tucked under his arm and plastered against him helped her assume the role.

After her alarm had gone off that morning, she'd almost assured herself that yesterday, and more specifically last night, had been part of a strange quasi-nightmare, but as soon as Ruark had breezed in wearing a cheery smile and looking quite satisfied with the world, she knew she hadn't dreamed a single minute.

Dinner, their bizarre conversation, agreeing to his marriage proposal—they had all actually taken place. And when he'd suggested they'd marry as soon as it could be arranged, she'd been half-afraid Ruark would whip a minister out of the closet by the time Henri served coffee and chocolate éclairs. She'd honestly believed she'd had at least a week, but a day? Why, she couldn't think of a suitable item in her closet to wear!

Her wedding garment aside, she would have one final evening to herself. After that, she'd be with Ruark in one capacity or another twenty-four seven, which would be enough to send her into a panic, if she were the panicky sort.

Idly, she wondered if he realized she wasn't a

social butterfly, didn't belong to any ladies' or civic groups, and didn't have any serious hobbies. She jogged for exercise, preferred quiet evenings at home or in the company of a few close friends, and had memorized the take-out phone numbers for nearly every restaurant within a two-mile radius of her apartment. If he was looking for a socialite, the proverbial Earth Mother, or Suzy Homemaker, he would be sorely disappointed.

Disappointing him concerned her, although why she should worry if she did or not, she didn't know. She was what she was, and he would have to deal with her flaws and idiosyncrasies just like everyone else.

Fortunately, by the time she'd come to those terms, Ruark was finishing his speech. "We'll expect you all there," he told the excited staff moments before he tugged her into his office.

"Next time, could you give me a few minutes to pull my thoughts together before you drop your bombshells?" she asked waspishly as soon as they were alone. "Or maybe you'd like me to run out and announce who you really are, *Your Royal Highness*."

"They'll find out tomorrow when we make our vows," he said, sounding unconcerned by her threat to expose his secret. "By the way, I need your house keys."

She eyed him suspiciously. "What for? I'll pack my own things, thank you very much."

"Hugh and Joachim need access to your home in order to install a security system."

"A security system?" she echoed. "Why?"

"Because it needs one," he informed her. "Until we decide how we're going to combine house-holds, we either have a state-of-the-art system in place or I hire more security. Considering your place is rather small, I can either station people outside or bring in an RV to use as their base of operation."

She shuddered, both from the thought of what the neighbors would think to the way he made it sound as if guarding her was a military exercise. The idea of anyone observing her every move, even for her own protection, was daunting and thoroughly foreign. She didn't like it. Better to have an electronic watchdog than a real one.

"My keys are in my locker. I'll get them."

She hurried out and, after dodging the gauntlet of well-wishers, returned a few minutes later. "Here," she said, dropping both the front and back door keys into his palm. "Anything else?"

"Not at the moment."

With that, she fled, hoping, *praying* for a patient she could tend to. Luckily, she walked past several cubicles with charts waiting in the bins outside the doors. Grabbing the first medical record like a lifeline, she focused her attention on her job, although she soon found herself fielding situations that went beyond her new responsibilities. Ruark had been adamant about handling the administrative issues himself, so she passed them off to him all day long.

"Dr Sutton, Dr Casey called in sick again. He needs someone to take his place."

"Tell Dr Thomas."

"Dr Sutton, Central Supply says we can't have three-cc syringes because they're back-ordered. What do we want, ones or tens?"

"Tens, but tell Dr Thomas."

"Dr Sutton, we have a patient who insists one of us misplaced his false teeth while he was here yesterday, but no one remembers a patient with dentures."

"Tell Dr Thomas."

Unfortunately, he bounced those same issues back at her. It wasn't his fault. He was still trying to find his footing, but it meant she dealt with the problems twice. She simply had to be patient until he learned the ins and outs of their department's management.

"Gina, where's the list of locum physicians?"

"File cabinet, top drawer."

"Gina, who's in charge of Central Supply?"

"Jessie Ames. Extension 4125."

Amazingly enough, he didn't ask her to look into the missing denture problem, so when she interrupted him for a patient consultation, she brought up the subject herself.

"Oh, that," he said when questioned. "He wasn't our patient. He'd gone to St Bridgit's, so I happily referred him over there."

St Bridgit's was a small hospital across town, about half the size of Belmont, but in spite of being Belmont's competitor, they shared a congenial working relationship.

"I'm glad it was them and not us," she commented, thinking of all the paperwork they'd been spared.

"Tell me about it," he said fervently, before he leaned back in his chair and steepled his fingers. "What's on your mind?"

Think of me as your husband first. Although he'd made that statement in regard to their hours spent privately, it was far too easy to think of him in that light every time she saw him. Perhaps once the shock wore off, she'd become better at compartmentalizing her life, but right now she was having difficulty separating Ruark, her future husband, from Ruark Thomas, her boss.

As his calm gaze met hers, she clutched the chart in her hand and forced herself to focus on her patient. "Roger Davis is sixty-three years old and has a history of type-two diabetes. He's been vomiting since yesterday morning and hasn't been able to keep anything down."

"Has he taken his insulin?"

"He claims he has." Gina ran through his symptoms. "He doesn't have fever, diarrhea, headache, achiness or chest pain. As expected, his electrolytes show he's slightly dehydrated so he's presently on IV fluids."

"Any history of GI problems?"

"None."

"Lab work?"

"Pending. His bedside glucose was 405, which is four times the normal. Critical, in fact."

"Food poisoning?"

"It's possible," she admitted. "Diabetics who are sick can have results in the two or three hundreds, but four hundred seems excessive for a simple case of food poisoning."

"Want me to take a look?" he asked.

"Would you mind?"

She escorted him to room two. Mr Davis sat on the edge of the bed, wearing a green Hawaiian-print shirt and pressed tan slacks. His dark brown hair was clearly courtesy of a toupee, but the IV in his hand, coupled with him retching into a plastic basin in his lap, spoiled the effect of a vacationing businessman.

"This is Dr Thomas," Gina announced. "And this is your lucky day. You get to see two of us for the price of one."

"I don't feel too lucky right now. In fact, I feel awful. Can't you do something to stop me heaving up my insides?"

"We're working on it," Ruark promised. "Are you able to keep anything down? Water? Tea?"

"Not for long."

"Are you having trouble urinating?"

"Haven't noticed, so I guess not."

He turned to Gina. "I want a urine sample."

"He already gave one. We're waiting for the lab report."

Ruark turned back to Roger. "Sit tight. We'll be right back."

He nodded right before another spate of retching struck. The two of them left him clutching his emesis basin.

"Any ideas?" she asked once they'd stepped into the hallway.

"I know it's easy for us to explain the unexplainable as a virus or food poisoning, but the other signs aren't there."

"I agree."

"He might have a urinary tract infection."

"I thought of that." She approached Ruby. "Check on Davis's urinalysis results, will you?"

Ruby handed her a page. "They came through a minute ago."

Gina scanned the document. "Bingo," she said before handing it to Ruark.

"The only problem is," he said slowly, "simple bladder infections don't cause vomiting, even in diabetics."

"What are you thinking?"

He shrugged. "Hard to say. His temperature, pulse and respirations are all normal, as is his blood pressure. How do you take temperatures here?"

"Ear probe."

"Can we get a rectal temp?"

"Sure, why not?" She waved at Lucy and made her request.

The nurse frowned as she listened, but she agreed to take the required temp. "I hope you aren't going to want these on everybody," she grumbled before she disappeared into Davis's cubicle. A few minutes later, she returned with a wide smile on her face. "It's 102."

"Then he *does* have a fever," Gina mused. "A urine infection, plus fever, plus vomiting adds up to—"

"Sepsis," Ruark finished.

Somehow, the bacteria invading Roger Davis's bladder had spread into his bloodstream and were attacking the man's natural defense systems. Left untreated, his blood vessels would collapse and his kidneys would fail.

Gina turned to Ruby. "Call the lab. I want stat blood cultures and then we're going to admit him." She faced Ruark and walked him back to his office. "A heavy dose of antibiotics is in order, wouldn't you say?"

He grinned. "Well done, Doctor."

She'd been set to congratulate herself on treating him as she would any other colleague, but before she could, he'd covered her hand with both of his. After Ruark's announcement, no one would comment or question if they were seen, but he was doing more than hold her hand. The small circles he traced in her palm nearly drove her crazy and caused her knees to grow weak. His touch sent a delicious shiver down her spine, but she found herself powerless to break contact.

And his eyes held such promise…such passion…and such frustration, as if he wanted to do much, much more….

Surprisingly enough, she wanted it, too. What was it about this man that he could so easily cause her to react like an infatuated teenager?

He'd said they'd take things slow and play having a physical relationship by ear. At this rate, they'd both be jiggling the bedsprings before the ink had dried on their marriage license.

"Same to you," she managed to say. "I wouldn't have considered taking a rectal temp."

He shrugged. "Sometimes you learn a few tricks. By the way, I forgot to tell you last night about Janice Myers."

His gentle caress befuddled her to the point where she had to forcibly think about who Janice Myers was. When she did, she was pleased her voice sounded normal, even though her pulse rate wasn't. "What did Horton find?"

A twinkle appeared in his eyes. "It was her appendix. Red, swollen, and ready to burst. If he'd delayed a few more hours, she'd be fighting peritonitis."

Gina's spirits soared. "I was right."

"And everyone knows it. From what I heard, Frank grumbled about doing the procedure from the time they wheeled her into the OR until he opened her up and it nearly jumped out at him. According to rumor, the nurses are hounding him to apologize, so be prepared."

She laughed, thrilled her instincts hadn't failed her. As much as she hated confrontation, arguing with the man had been worth every tense moment. "OK, but I won't hold my breath. Meanwhile, do you want to tell our patient his good news?"

"Go ahead. I have a ton of paperwork to finish before our date tonight."

"Our date?" she repeated.

"Sure. I thought we'd go to dinner."

"Sorry," she shook her head. "It's bad luck for the groom to see the bride before the wedding."

"I thought that applied to the day of the ceremony."

"Could be," she admitted, "but I have a hundred and one things to do before tomorrow."

"Then it's a good thing I've changed the schedule so we both have the next couple of days off. It won't be the longest of honeymoons, but we'll still have one."

Her face warmed as she'd hadn't given thought to anything other than the ceremony. In fact, she would have probably reported for her shift the next day as usual. So much for presenting the picture of wedded bliss. Suddenly, what they were about to do, and the ramifications if they— *she*—took a false step and committed a social error, overwhelmed her.

He shook his head and smiled. "Can't have the newlyweds working the day after, can we?"

She managed a smile. "Honestly? I hadn't thought about it."

"I have," he said firmly.

"Yes, but I didn't. And there's the problem." She tried to tug her hand free, but he didn't release it.

"I don't see one."

"Then you aren't looking. It's as plain as the nose on your face." She met his gaze, certain he would read the sorrow in her eyes. "This isn't going to work."

He frowned, before he pulled her into the nearest empty exam room. "Why do you say that?" he asked as soon as he'd closed the door and blocked it with his foot.

"Because I'm going to make a mistake and we won't convince anyone that this marriage isn't a farce," she wailed, tears threatening at the prospect of dragging her father's name through the proverbial mud when she failed. "The schedule is a prime example. I would have come on duty the next day and not thought a thing about it."

"Do you honestly believe I wouldn't have noticed if you'd gotten up at 5:00 a.m.? That I wouldn't have stopped you?"

He sounded incredulous, and hearing him state it like that she felt a twinge of embarrassment before she squared her shoulders and looked him straight in the eye.

"The point is, you would have had to stop me. What happens when you aren't around to correct my blunders? I'll do or say something that will raise questions and then—"

"You're being too hard on yourself," he told her. "In a few days you'll settle into a new routine and you'll be fine."

"And if I'm not?"

"Then everyone will believe my wife is a dizzy blonde and will feel sorry for me," he said soberly.

She narrowed her eyes as his comment sank in. "Did you call me a dizzy blonde?" Then, as soon as she saw his smile, she knew he'd only been trying to end her pity party, and he'd succeeded. She punched him playfully in his biceps.

"Those are fighting words," she said without heat.

"Noted. As for making mistakes, I hear it's a common phenomenon among newlyweds. After my brother's wedding, he introduced his wife to the German ambassador as his girlfriend, which caused more than a few chuckles, although my sister-in-law didn't find it as humorous as we did."

"I'm sure she didn't."

"The point is, don't worry."

Easier said than done, but his confidence was infectious. "Is that a royal decree?" she asked lightly.

"Absolutely." He tipped her chin up so their gazes met. "Better?"

She nodded. "Yeah. Thanks."

With a feather-light touch, he tucked a lock of her hair behind one ear before he lowered his head and kissed her.

It began softly, tentatively, then became more

demanding and certain. He pulled her against him and the heat from his body penetrated her scrub suit and heavy lab coat.

He nibbled on her lower lip and she opened her mouth to tease him in kind before the soft, erotic touch of their tongues meeting made her burst into flames.

Instinctively, she threaded her arms around his neck and stood on tiptoe to press herself against him. His lips moved from her mouth to her cheek, then to her ear, before trailing down her neck. She leaned her head back, eager to offer more of herself to him, until she heard voices outside.

He must have, too, because he instantly stilled, then loosened his hold on her and grinned.

"Do not say a word," she ordered as she ran her hands through her hair and checked her clothing. Nothing seemed amiss, so she flung open the door.

"Gina?" he called.

"What?" She paused on the threshold, irritated by her enthusiastic response as much as she was awed by his kiss.

"You look…" He paused, then smiled.

Once again, she checked herself. "You were saying?"

"Now you look 'engaged'."

Gina clutched the bouquet of flowers Ruark had given her prior to their wedding ceremony in a near death-grip, conscious of Ruark—her *husband!*—following her into his home around ten o'clock the next evening. He looked exceedingly handsome in his black tuxedo and she could imagine how breathtaking he would be if he'd worn his official state dress, complete with ribbons, sashes and sword. Clothes may not make the man, but they certainly dazzled feminine eyes.

And while their wedding had been an impromptu affair, she was glad she'd chosen this calf-length lacy white dress that swirled so invitingly around her legs instead of the business suit she'd initially planned to buy. She hadn't felt this feminine since the last formal ball she'd attended as a med student.

"The ceremony and reception afterward turned out well, didn't it?" she asked as she stood in the hallway and wondered where to go next.

He raised one eyebrow. "Did you expect otherwise?"

"To be honest, I didn't know *what* I was expecting," she admitted. "You truly thought of everything."

He had. The hospital chaplain had performed the ceremony as the thirty guests filled the chapel to capacity. Afterwards, they'd gone to a conference room for a small reception with the required cake and punch. A chamber ensemble had provided the music and a short, homely fellow had bustled around, taking photographs until she'd hardly been able to see anything except spots. Someone had decorated the chapel and the reception room using the same mixed flower theme as in her bouquet.

Somehow Ruark had even managed to book an appointment with her hairdresser and a manicurist for earlier in the day.

She couldn't think of a thing that had been missed. No one could accuse them of shortchanging their wedding—other than the bride and groom not being in love, of course.

Don't think about that, she scolded herself. *You knew what you were agreeing to, as well as Ruark's feelings on the subject. You can't look back. Only forward.*

"I tried," he said as an embarrassed grin

appeared. "We're only doing this once so I wanted you to have all the trappings."

Touched by his effort to make this day as special as possible under the circumstances, a lump formed unexpectedly in her throat. "Thank you," she whispered.

"Before you credit me with all the details, I should probably admit my staff reminded me of a few things and handled most of the legwork. The guest book, bows on the pews." He shrugged. "Things like that."

"Regardless, you did a remarkable job on such short notice. Frankly, you delivered more than I expected. Maybe you should go into the wedding planning business," she said lightly, holding her slightly wilted bouquet like a talisman. "You're wasted as a physician."

He visibly shuddered. "Sorry. Give me a trauma, not color schemes and cake flavors."

"Speaking of cake, it was delicious." To be honest, she hadn't actually tasted it until her last two bites, but those two bites had been exquisite.

"Thank Henri. He's been creating since you left the other night," he admitted on a wry note. "He insisted on white but knows I prefer chocolate, so he baked one of each."

"I'll speak to him," she promised.

Ruark loosened his bow-tie and shrugged off his jacket. "I shouldn't be hungry, but I am. Want to raid the refrigerator?"

Her stomach still hadn't settled from her nervous excitement, but sitting in the kitchen appealed far more than unpacking her suitcase or going straight to bed. "Sure, why not?"

But once they'd entered Henri's domain and found him packaging the remnants of their reception for the freezer, he waved his arms and dismissed them.

"What man thinks of food on his wedding night?" the Frenchman chided.

Ruark winked at Gina. "A hungry one."

Henri tutted before promising to bring a tray upstairs, his florid face beaming at the couple. "Now, shoo. Go and enjoy each other."

Literally pushed out of the room, the chef's comment seemed to echo in the empty dining hall. *Enjoy each other.*

For some reason, she found the Frenchman's instructions sweet, although from Ruark's disconcerted expression he did not.

"Does he know about—?" she began.

"Yes, but he's a romantic at heart. So, shall we

adjourn upstairs, as we've been commanded?" he said dryly. "Or head for the study to watch television?"

She wasn't ready to enter his bedroom so she chose the alternative. "The study," she answered promptly.

But once there she was too keyed up to focus on world events, the weather forecast, or the current baseball standings. She strolled around the room and noticed the eight-by-ten framed portrait of his family on his desk. It was an official photo because the men wore ribbons, sashes and swords, and the women wore ballgowns, diamonds and rubies. What struck her most was how closely the men resembled each other.

"Tell me about your family," she said, hoping to hear they were like everyone else underneath their royal trappings.

He joined her at his desk. "This is my father, Frederick." He pointed to the distinguished-looking gentleman wearing a gold crown. "He's been the King of Marestonia for the last fifteen years since my grandfather died. My mother, Christina, is from Sweden and stays busy with her charity work. When she's not traveling or fund-raising, she's busy with our family and state events. Don't worry, though, she'll welcome you with open arms."

"I see." She hadn't met the woman and Gina was already intimidated by her activities and accomplishments.

"This is my oldest brother, George. He's married and has two children, both girls, with another baby on the way."

"Boy or girl?"

"The last I knew, they refused to reveal the baby's sex. I suspect it's a boy because George seems to smirk more than usual these days." He grinned. "He's always been the doting papa, though, so I could be wrong.

"Pieter is next. He's quite serious about a young lawyer friend, but they haven't issued any formal announcements as yet."

Which explained why the duty of marrying her had fallen on Ruark.

"I'm third in line and I'm sure you recognize me."

She did, although he looked far more imposing in the photo than in real life.

"The twins are my sisters Beatrix and Mary. Bea is working on her Master's degree in international finance and Mary is finishing her training as a physical therapist." He grinned. "Much to my mother's dismay, both of them are, as you say, footloose and fancy-free."

"High-spirited, are they?"

"No, just not married. My mother wants more grandchildren."

"But she has two already and another on the way."

"My mother won't be satisfied until we've all given her at least two. Have you ever considered how many you'd like to have?"

She grinned. "Grandchildren? I really haven't thought about it."

"Children," he corrected.

"I always dreamed of having four."

"Four?"

"Sure. Two boys, two girls, so each would have a playmate. But it really doesn't matter how many or their sex, as long as they're healthy. What about you?"

"I haven't given the numbers much thought," he admitted before his eyes took on a decided gleam. "I'm more interested in the activities that lead up to having kids."

"Naturally," she said dryly. Then, because the conversation seemed to be traveling in a direction she wasn't prepared to go, she replaced the frame on his desk and returned to the sofa.

There, she kicked off her shoes, dug her toes into the plush carpeting, toyed with her charm bracelet and wondered how she'd manage to sleep with her husband lying beside her—a husband who wasn't interested in a celibate relationship.

After yesterday's stolen kiss in the exam room, she'd been torn between anticipation and dread about this moment. She'd asked for time, but she was only prolonging the inevitable. It wasn't as if she had to manufacture sparks— she could feel them now and he wasn't even within touching distance. And yet, because love wasn't part of the formula of their marriage, wouldn't getting to know each other before becoming intimate make the experience that much better?

Out of the corner of her eye she noticed how carefully he watched the announcers, as if engrossed in every word they said. Irrationally, his attitude irritated her. How could he be so calm and so focused on sports at a time like this?

"Do you play chess?" he asked abruptly.

"It's been a long time," she admitted, releasing her bracelet with a snap.

"Can I interest you in a game?"

She would have agreed to anything. "If you don't mind a rusty opponent, I'd love one."

He pulled a well-used set out of a cupboard and

placed it on a small table in the far left corner. "Black or white?" he asked.

"White," she answered.

"Black is my lucky color," he said as he arranged his side of the board.

"White is mine, so look out."

By the time Henri arrived with a tray of champagne, grapes, various cheeses and chocolate-dipped strawberries, Ruark had captured most of her pieces.

"Chess?" The chef frowned as he placed the snacks on the nearby coffee table. "On your wedding night?"

Ruark glared at the fellow and signaled for him to leave. He could think of other, far more pleasurable activities they could be doing without the chef's well-meant interference, but he wasn't about to explain there was method in his madness. After watching Gina fidget for the last twenty minutes, he had to do something to help her relax. While he would prefer a more personal technique, a game of chess would work nicely to divert attention away from her fears.

As Henri silently exited, Ruark captured her queen.

"Darn!" Gina muttered, a cute little wrinkle appearing on her forehead.

He grinned. "Don't lose heart. You still have your king."

While she contemplated her next move, Ruark watched her. The way she worried her lower lip with her teeth, drummed her fingers on the tabletop while touching the heads of her pieces with the other, amused him. She seemed determined not to let him win, or at least not win easily. True, she was a little rusty, as she'd claimed, but if they played on a regular basis, it wouldn't be long before she became a formidable opponent.

A few moves later, he pronounced, "Checkmate," and the game was over.

Gina leaned back in her chair. "I demand a rematch."

"OK, but first Henri's refreshments are waiting." He eyed the platter. "Good thing, because I'm starved."

He probably wouldn't have been if he'd taken time for the light meal Henri had prepared before the ceremony, but after reading the latest news from Marestonia on the Internet, food had been the least of his worries. Making their marriage official had been all he'd cared about. He'd been ninety-nine percent sure Gina wouldn't cry off, but that final one percentage point had nagged at him until he'd seen her at the back of the chapel.

He'd never known relief like at that moment.

He retrieved the champagne and handed a glass to Gina. "How about a strawberry?"

"I'd love one." She bit into the fruit he offered.

"You really don't play all that badly," he said, taking a strawberry for himself. "Did your father teach you?"

"Yes, although I'm not doing justice to his instructions." She chuckled. "When I said I was rusty, I didn't know I was *this* awful. I'm rather embarrassed."

"Would you rather try your luck at something else? Cards, backgammon, poker?" Oh, the possibilities of poker…

"I prefer chess, unless you're tired of my novice skills."

He grinned. "As long as I win, I don't mind."

Two games later, with the food nearly gone and the wins all Ruark's, Gina yawned. "One more match," she begged.

He shook his head, quite aware of his wife's reluctance to go upstairs. "You're half-asleep. You can see if you can best me tomorrow." He tugged her to her feet. "Run along. I'll be there shortly."

She nodded, then padded from the room as her dress swooshed gently with each step. After seeing her only in shapeless scrub suits, the moment she'd walked into the chapel wearing a dress that clung to her slight curves and revealed a pair of shapely legs, he'd been stunned. His imagination definitely hadn't done her justice. And knowing that, he'd been hard pressed not to stare at her like a besotted fool.

He downed the last of the champagne, wishing he'd imbibed enough to fall asleep the moment his head hit the pillow. How would he manage to keep his hands to himself as promised, when her light, floral scent tantalized him and her softness called his name?

Fifteen minutes later, after stalling as long as he could, he flicked off the light switches and trudged upstairs in a state of combined anticipation and frustrated dread.

In his room, he found Gina already in his four-poster bed, the sheet pulled to her waist. She'd left the bedside lamp on for him—such a wifely act—and he caught a glimpse of her negligee's lacy bodice and the bare skin above it.

Determined to act naturally in spite of his body's immediate response, he stripped down to his shorts, flicked off the light, then slid into bed.

For several moments, he lay there, as stiff as a board, aware of Gina doing the same, before he reached a decision.

He rolled toward her, raised himself on one elbow and said, "Gina?"

"Yes." Her voice sounded tentative.

"You were beautiful tonight."

He heard the smile in her voice. "Thank you. You were quite handsome and dashing yourself."

He scooted closer and felt tension radiating off her. "If you don't relax, you'll wake up stiff and sore in the morning."

Her soft sigh made him smile. "Probably."

"So, in the interests of our health…" In a lightning-fast move, he slid one arm under her neck and positioned her against him as he settled onto his back.

She gasped, one hand splayed across his chest. "What…what are you doing?"

He bussed her cheek. "Holding my wife so we can both sleep. Goodnight, Gina."

"Goodnight, Ruark."

For the next few minutes, he waited for a sign

to indicate she'd fallen asleep, but none came. Her breathing hadn't changed and she wiggled every so often as if to find a comfortable position.

Her hand stroked his abdominal muscles and he gritted his teeth in a vain attempt to maintain control. What in the world had he been thinking? This whole exercise was to allow her to adjust to being in his bed, not drive him over the edge with desire.

As Ruark lay beside her, his promise warred with his hormones, but he forced himself to freeze. Although he wanted to bury himself inside her, he wouldn't because he couldn't bear to see the wounded look in her eyes if he did. He'd made a vow to her and pride demanded he honor it.

"Ruark?" she asked softly.

"Yeah." His voice was hoarse.

"Did we do the right thing?"

Concentrating on holding his body in check, he didn't follow her question. "With what?"

"Getting married. Especially under our circumstances. Was it the right thing to do?"

Aware of her body plastered against his and the frustration he was suffering, he wondered that himself. No, he decided. Getting married wasn't the problem. Giving her time to adjust to the concept of having a husband and everything it entailed was.

He couldn't complain, though, because he'd brought this on himself with his momentary lapse into chivalry!

"It was." He was certain.

"Convince me," she said.

CHAPTER SEVEN

RUARK stilled. "Convince you?" he echoed.

She shifted her position until she was half-draped across his body and one smooth leg had found its way between his. "Yes."

He didn't want to misunderstand and start something he wouldn't be allowed to finish, so he restated her request. "You want me to convince you that we did the right thing by getting married."

"The circumstances *were* rather unusual," she pointed out. "I know we married out of duty, for the good of the people in two countries, but I just want some reassurance the result wasn't a mistake."

His confused fog lifted. "You mean, a mistake for *us*. Personally."

"Yeah."

She obviously wasn't able to put her fears into words or was too afraid of his answer if she did. Oh, he knew what she wanted to hear—it was the same thing *every* woman wanted. They expected flowery speeches and the I-can't-live-without-you-because-I-love-you remarks, but he owed her complete honesty. At this point, he certainly couldn't profess to love her and probably never would. Love, as far as he was concerned, was simply a euphemism for lust, and he had plenty of that where she was concerned.

"We did what we had to do," he stated firmly. "A lot of people will benefit from this marriage, true. We knew that going into it. But we're bene-fitting, too."

She didn't comment, but he sensed she was lis-tening carefully. "We each have someone to share our lives with," he said simply. "Someone who'll listen and be supportive, someone to come home to at night."

Realizing how his description could also apply to a pet, which hadn't been his intention, he grinned and tried to lighten the mood. "Someone who prefers white cake and leaves all the choco-late for me."

She chuckled. "If you say so."

"Someone I can beat at chess."

"Give me a few weeks to practice and then we'll see who beats who," she said without heat.

"Regardless of who wins, chess is something enjoyable we can do together. Best of all, we won't have to find a date ever again, much less suffer through the rejections and heartbreaks."

She laughed. "You? Rejected? Heartbroken? Oh, please. I'm sure it was the other way around."

"*Au contraire.*"

"Do you want to talk about it?"

He didn't, but felt he should. Perhaps once he explained, Gina would understand why he held the opinions he did. "This is ancient history, mind you."

"How ancient?"

He shrugged. "Seven, eight years, but it started long before then. Having a title gets in the way of a relationship. It's tough to find a woman who doesn't have an agenda or who can look past my heritage to the man underneath. I learned to be cautious."

"Royalty 101?"

"Something like that."

"But someone slipped past your defenses."

"Yeah." He rubbed his chin. "I met this woman during my residency. To me, Grace was perfect. I loved her and she loved me. Or so she claimed."

"Claimed?"

"We dated for several months. One day she said

she loved me, but two weeks later someone better came along, and she left."

"Someone better? How is that possible? You're a prince, for heaven's sake."

He grinned. "Spoken like a loyal wife. Anyway, her 'someone better' was a movie producer who could advance her career more than a prince who practically lived at the hospital. It was my own fault because I should have seen it coming."

"I didn't realize you can predict events."

"The signs were in plain sight, but I ignored them. You see, we didn't have anything in common. Other than attending charity events or her movie opening nights, we led separate lives."

"Have you seen her lately?"

"No. Last I heard, she was on her third marriage and still waiting for her big break."

Gina fell silent as she searched for something appropriate to say. Discussing his former love life while he was in bed with her could be considered tacky, but sometimes it was easier to reveal things in the dead of night rather than in the light of day. In any case, hearing of his experiences explained so much. Now Gina understood why he had such a cynical view about love, why he continued to stress the importance of having mutual interests, of being companions, of sharing a life.

She snuggled against him. "I wish I could feel sorry for this Grace person, but I can't. Anyway, enough about her. I want to hear more about *our* personal benefits."

"More personal benefits. OK, let me think. Here's one. I don't have to worry about choosing the wrong tie because you'll tell me what matches and what doesn't. And I'll reciprocate when you choose the wrong earrings for your dress."

"Fair enough. What else?"

"You have a French chef preparing the most delectable meals on this side of the Mississippi while I won't have to argue with Henri over the menus any longer."

"Something's not quite right with that one, but I'll let it slide," she said dryly, smiling. "Is that all you have?"

"Well…we can share transportation to and from work to save on energy costs," he finished brightly.

"Now you're reaching."

"Yes, but I'm saving the best for last." He moved his head to whisper in her ear. "I find you extremely, *extremely* beautiful, Gina." His voice became rougher, almost raspy, as if he was using all of his energy to keep from acting on that attraction. "And you're my wife," he finished on a distinct note of possessiveness.

She, on the other hand, was grateful the room was too dark for him to see her grinning like an idiot. "I'm flattered."

She felt his shrug. "It's the truth."

"In that case…for the record…the feeling is mutual." There, she'd said it! At the same time, though, she sensed his appeal went beyond his handsome face and his ability to turn her inside out with a mere kiss. She may not have known him for long, but she'd caught glimpses of his character that were as much if not more alluring.

She may not appreciate being married out of duty, but once she'd gotten past the shock and analyzed his motives, his willingness to place other people's needs above his own—his *unselfishness*—she'd been impressed. And when he'd stood behind her with her incident with Frank Horton, when he'd done all he could to give her a wedding ceremony she'd never forget, how could she *not* be attracted to him on more than a physical level?

The question was, what should she do about it? Postpone the inevitable, or allow her wedding day—and night—to be everything it should be? What had he said? People wouldn't care how their romance started, only how it ended?

Why couldn't she heed Henri's advice to enjoy each other? Considering their shared physical attraction, their joining was as inevitable as the sun rising and setting.

"We'll only have one wedding night," she said, hoping he'd hear the invitation in her voice.

Obviously he had, because he froze. "True," he admitted. "But you wanted to wait."

"I changed my mind."

"Once we start, there's no going back," he warned.

"I know. I won't regret this in the morning," she stated firmly, but he still didn't move. "If you're afraid I've drunk too much champagne and don't know what I'm saying, rest easy. I only had one glass."

Determined to convince him of her sincerity, she reached up to cup the side of his face. "You said we'd play this part of our marriage by ear. Well, I heard the music and now I'm ready to dance."

In an instant he'd reversed positions until she was half-undereath him. She sensed rather than saw him lower his head until his lips touched her cheek. Slowly, deliberately, provocatively, he nibbled his way to her ear and trailed his lips down her neck until he reached her collarbone. "Shall we tango...or waltz?" he mumbled against her skin.

"Both."

Time froze under his tender assault. The nightgown she'd purchased that morning disappeared, unneeded and unwanted. Each long stroke, every caress pulled her deeper under his magical spell. Oh, yes, she managed to think...their marriage may have been born out of duty and would be scrutinized by many, but nights like this were not a mistake.

"Your Highness, you must allow me to prepare your breakfast."

Caught in the act of pouring a packet of instant oatmeal into a bowl, Gina smiled at Henri, who'd burst into the kitchen with a look of horror on his face. "Don't be ridiculous. I'm perfectly able to fix my own."

"Of course you are, but it is my pleasure to serve you," the chef said smoothly as he waved her aside. "Would you like toast, fresh fruit, bacon and eggs to accompany this?"

"Just the oatmeal," she told him. "And a refill

of this." She raised her mug. "It's the best I've ever tasted."

When she'd awoken that morning, she'd only seen Ruark's indented pillow and a cup of coffee on her nightstand. She normally didn't take time to brew any at home before she reported for her shift and, in fact, didn't need the shot of caffeine to start her day, but having a cup ready and waiting when her eyes popped open would definitely spoil her.

Henri beamed as he grabbed the pot and topped up her cup. "Thank you, Your Highness. I'll bring your breakfast to the dining room shortly."

Clearly dismissed, Gina meandered into the dining room and sat at the huge banquet-sized table. Within minutes Henri delivered a bowl of oatmeal sprinkled with fresh blueberries. He'd also brought a plate of assorted fruit and two slices of whole wheat toast cut in perfect triangles, as well as the morning newspaper.

"Let me know if I can prepare anything else, Your Highness."

"This will be all. Tell me, has Ruark already eaten?"

"Hours ago, ma'am. He's an early riser," Henri explained. "I heard him mention he had correspondence to attend to, so I'm certain he's in his den if you're wondering where to find him."

She was, but didn't want to interrupt him. "Thank you, Henri."

Accustomed to eating alone, she perused the headlines, ate half of what Henri had supplied, then headed for her bedroom. She hadn't made the bed or tidied the room yet, and she still had two suitcases' worth of clothes to unpack.

To her surprise, she found a woman her own age performing all the chores Gina had planned to do after breakfast. The bed was made, the room tidied, and her suitcases were open and half-empty.

"You didn't need to do this for me!" Gina exclaimed, disconcerted to have someone else doing such personal tasks.

"It is my job, Your Highness. I'm happy to do it. I am Inga, by the way. I usually come three days a week to help Mrs Armstrong, but now I'll be here every day."

Mrs Armstrong was the kindly housekeeper responsible for the house's pristine condition, which couldn't have been easy considering the number of people who lived and worked on the property. While Gina was glad the woman had help and Inga had a full-time job, she hoped no one thought she was too lazy to lend a hand or, worse, had extremely high housekeeping standards. As far as she was concerned, a house wasn't complete without several dust bunnies in residence.

Gina watched Inga hang up a pink blouse in the closet. "Thank you, Inga," she said politely. "I'll try not to make too much of a mess for you. Meanwhile, I'll get out of your way."

"The garden flowers are lovely right now," Inga commented. "Perhaps you'd like to see them before the day gets too hot?"

She couldn't hang around the kitchen or her bedroom, and she didn't want to interrupt Ruark, so strolling around the yard seemed a good idea. If she was lucky, she might even find a few weeds to pull. "I will."

But outside the rose bushes were perfectly pruned, the zinnias, petunias, and vinca were well watered, and the small herb garden beautifully tended. Not a weed was in sight, thanks to the two employees who sported *Gary's Gardens* on the back of their uniform shirts.

She sank onto a wicker chair under the covered patio and studied the professionally landscaped yard, wondering what she would do for the next three days. Monday wouldn't come soon enough to suit her. At least at the hospital, she had a place. In Ruark's home, she was beginning to feel like a useless ornament.

A few minutes later, her new husband strolled outside. "Here you are."

"Yup, here I am," she replied.

He sat in the chair opposite hers. "Have you found your way around? Met all the staff?"

"Oh, yes. They're delightful. Very helpful and eager to serve." That was the problem. She wasn't used to having her every whim catered to. It would take some time to adjust, especially being referred to as "Your Highness".

"Good." He placed her well-used electronic PDA in front of her—the same one she carried in her pocket as a reference guide for all sorts of treatment protocols and drug information. "I apologize for taking this off your dresser without your permission this morning, but you were asleep and I didn't want to wake you."

She hadn't noticed but, then, she hadn't looked for it either. "No problem."

"My secretary updated the calendar with our social engagements. I thought we could review them together."

She navigated the screen to reach the current

month. "An interview with *Modern Marestonians*." She glanced at him. "In two *days*?"

"The magazine is a sort of cross between your *Country Living* and *People*. It has a large readership and their reporters tend to be quite congenial. Perfect for your first interview."

"Thanks," she said wryly, then glanced down at the screen again. "A charity event on Friday night?"

"For family crisis centers in the state," he explained. "The numbers of safe havens for victims of domestic violence and their children isn't meeting the demand, unfortunately."

After seeing many of those victims in the ER, the subject was dear to Gina's heart, and she approved of his decision to support the cause. She glanced at the next entry.

"A ribbon-cutting ceremony?"

"For a regional burns center in Chicago."

"Chicago? That's hours away."

"Not by private plane," he informed her. "It won't take any longer than if we drove across town."

Ribbon-cuttings, jetting around the Midwest, an official royal event every week. Obviously his princely duties rolled around more than the few times a year as he'd originally claimed, and she said so.

"We'll be busy for a while because we're news at the moment," he admitted. "Before long, we'll be usurped by an actress arrested for driving under the influence or a politician divorcing his wife because he's gay."

His light-hearted reassurance coaxed a grin out of her. "Do you think we'll be that lucky?"

"Count on it." His tone grew serious. "Just remember, I'll be right beside you."

"You'd better be," she warned, "because I don't have a clue what to say."

"I'll handle it," he promised. "All you have to do is look beautiful and smile like a blushing bride."

A blushing bride. She chose not to point out that brides blushed as a result of their husband's love and as that emotion didn't apply… But considering how far out of her depth she was, she hoped a reporter would attribute her uncertainty at being in the spotlight to her newlywed status.

"Any questions?" he asked.

"About this interview on Sunday," she began. "What sort of questions will she ask?"

"As no one in our country really knows you, she'll be interested in your childhood, your parents, your education. And, of course, in light of events back home, she'll want to see how we're reconciling the past with the present. Just follow my lead and you'll be fine."

"So you say," she muttered.

"It will get easier," he assured her. "I'm fortunate in that my life is really quite boring in comparison to the rest of the royal family's, so the press normally leaves me alone. As soon as talk of our wedding dies down, we'll be practically invisible."

Being invisible couldn't come soon enough, Gina thought as she studied her reflection in the full-length mirror on Sunday afternoon. Ever since the announcement of their marriage, gifts had flooded into their home and Ruark's secretary had been inundated with requests for photos and interviews. To her relief, he freely supplied pictures and rarely granted an audience. She hoped to survive today's session without incident.

It was important for everything to go well because so much rested on the way she presented herself as Ruark's wife. The news from Avelogne and Marestonia over the past couple of days had shown two countries in a state of uncertainty. The mood ranged from hopeful to skeptical about the alliance between their two royal houses, but the violence had stopped, which the political gurus took as a positive sign. However, Gina hadn't needed Ruark or the Marestonian ambassador to tell her how fragile the peace actually was. It was her job during today's interview to convince everyone of their modern-day fairy-tale romance.

A tall order considering how Ruark scoffed at the concept of love and they'd simply married to fulfill a duty.

Duty, not love.

Suddenly, guilt crashed down on her. The past nights in his bed had been wonderful, spectacular even, but they weren't in love. What did it say about her character, her morals, if she could find such enjoyment in the arms of a man who didn't feel anything for her?

Worse yet, what did it say about *her* character if *she* could do the same?

Her guilt turned to horrified shame as she considered how easily she'd succumbed to his charm.

"My, but you look beautiful." Ruark came from the bathroom and adjusted his tie.

Staggering under the weighty question that plagued her, she managed to answer. "Thanks."

He stopped beside her, tall and handsome in his dark gray suit, his frown plain in the mirror's reflection. "What's wrong? Do you feel all right?"

"I'm fine," she insisted. *As fine as any woman who saw a distasteful quality inside herself.*

His frown didn't disappear as he felt her forehead. "You don't look fine."

"Thank you very much for your observation," she said dryly.

"I'm serious. If you're getting sick, you should rest. We can reschedule."

The warmth of his fingers calmed her as much as his obvious concern did, and her momentary guilt and shame vanished. Regardless of the practical reasons behind their marriage, they *were* married. Being married, for better or worse, made it pointless not to find joy in their relationship wherever they could.

She may not feel the grand passion she'd always imagined, but she trusted him, respected him, and enjoyed his company. She had nothing to feel ashamed about. And, if she was honest with herself, he was a man she could easily grow to love.

Oh, who was she kidding? Her intuition said she was halfway there.

As for Ruark, he may not love her, but he clearly cared about her. She'd seen him express concern under a veneer of polite interest—his royal persona—but this was different. His worry was genuine and obviously heartfelt if the look on his face was anything to go by. It might not be the stuff of hearts and roses, but for now it was enough. And with time and patience it might eventually grow into something close to what her parents had.

"No, don't reschedule. I'm just...nervous, I guess. When I think of how our every expression and tone will be scrutinized..."

"Act naturally and the reporter will simply see a happily married couple who've given up a few hours of their precious honeymoon to share their story."

She laughed. "Precious?"

"When you only have three days, every moment counts. Seriously, though, just be yourself."

"Be myself. Got it," she said, pretending confidence when she had none. "But she'll be sorely disappointed once she realizes I think and act like a physician, not a princess."

"But now you are both. I think this will help." He strode across the room to his dresser, opened the top drawer, and pulled out a large, square jeweler's box. "For you."

Her heart pounded with excitement. "What is it?"

"A gift from my parents."

"Your parents? It isn't a tiara or some other princessy thing, is it?" she asked suspiciously, wondering if she'd commit a horrible breach of royal etiquette if she refused to wear it for their interview.

He laughed. "Tiaras are reserved for state events so, no, it isn't. This, however, is something I hope you'll like. It arrived last night." As she hesitated, he urged, "Go ahead. Open it."

She raised the hinged lid to reveal a sparkling teardrop diamond pendant resting on a bed of velvet. She may have had a novice eye when it came to gems, but the size suggested it was horribly expensive. "It's beautiful."

He removed the pendant from the box, then fastened the silver chain around her neck. "This was my mother's. She asks you to wear it with her blessing. My father gave it to her on the day I was born."

Touched by the generosity of his mother, tears threatened to fall as she fingered the diamond's facets. "It's gorgeous. Thank you, and thank your mother for sharing it with me."

"I'm glad you like it." His smile seemed rooted in relief, as if he'd been afraid she would reject a gift that held special significance to him and his family. "But I'll let you thank her yourself."

"I will." She'd spoken to Ruark's parents the morning after their wedding when they'd welcomed her into the family. Their voices had been warm and sincere, and Gina was looking forward to meeting the couple in person, as well as the rest of Ruark's family.

"She's quite anxious for a lengthy chat," he added. "Probably so she can warn you about all my bad habits."

So far, she hadn't noted a single one but, then, they'd only been living together for three days. "Gracious." She pretended horror. "How many do you have?"

"Hundreds, I'm sure. Probably more, depending on who you ask." He grinned.

"Regardless of what she tells me, I'll always treasure this," she said before she stood on tiptoe and pressed her lips lightly against his for just long enough to taste the coffee on his breath.

A lazy half-smile appeared on his face and his eyes gleamed with masculine appreciation. "Remind me to give gifts more often," he said in a lazy drawl. "Even if they aren't my own."

She chuckled at his hopeful expression. "Don't push your luck."

"At the risk of spoiling the moment, after we

talk to my parents tonight, your grandmother would appreciate a phone call."

She stiffened instinctively. "I'm sure she would, but I'm not ready."

"You don't have to agree to meet her. Just talk."

"I wouldn't know what to say."

"You could start by thanking her for the gift she sent."

A white linen tablecloth had arrived, exquisitely hand-stitched with the royal crests from both families. It was beautiful, a true work of textile art, and a host of poor souls had probably worked round the clock to create it once she'd agreed to marry Ruark. Either that, or her grandmother had been so certain of the outcome to the royal plan that she'd commissioned it some months ago.

"I'll send a card."

"She wants to visit—at our convenience, of course."

"Sometimes life doesn't give us what we want."

"You can't hold a grudge forever."

"I don't have a grudge. I don't feel…anything." As far as Gina was concerned, she might share a gene pool with the woman, but she was simply a name. Another famous person she would never meet. A complete stranger.

A few short days ago, so was Ruark.

Yes, and look where that had gotten her. She was now his wife.

She slowly exhaled, feeling Ruark's scrutiny. "I appreciate you acting as a mediator, but I'm not ready," she repeated. "She'll have to be content that I agreed to their plan when I could have ignored Avelogne's problems."

He started to speak, then stopped as if he knew she wouldn't budge no matter how hard he pushed. "It's your decision, but keep in mind she isn't getting any younger."

She would have replied, but the doorbell chimed in the distance. Adrenaline surged and panic instantly set in. "Oh, my gosh. She's here, and she's *early*."

Ruark threaded her arm through his and pulled her close. "Look at it this way. You'll have less time to brood."

"Brood? I don't brood. It makes me sound like a chicken," she mumbled as he led her into the hallway toward the staircase.

"You aren't a chicken," he agreed. "You're braver than that."

"Do you think so?"

"Absolutely."

She stopped at the top of the stairs. "Maybe I should change into something more sophisticated, less—"

He tugged on her arm and she followed. "You look fantastic."

Three steps later, she stopped again. "What if she asks a question I can't answer?"

"Squeeze my hand and I'll take over."

"Any other final bits of advice?"

"Remember to smile and look like you adore me."

He winked playfully, and she burst out laughing. "If you insist. One case of adoration coming up."

By the time Ruark had gotten Gina to the bottom of the staircase, he'd accomplished what he'd set out to do—he'd wiped the startled doe-in-the-headlights look off her face. Louise Amandine's first impression of his wife would show her as a relaxed and happy bride.

As the interview progressed, the experienced reporter was far more interested in Gina than in him, which suited Ruark just fine. People in his part of the world clamored to learn everything possible about the new princess, especially because no one had gleaned more than her basic historical facts. He rather enjoyed sitting next to Gina in the formal parlor, holding her hand like an enamored husband as he listened to her share stories and anecdotes about her childhood and her parents.

He was an extremely lucky man, he decided. For a man who'd married only to appease his family's honor, who thought love was an over-rated emotion, he was very fortunate to have married a woman he actually liked and enjoyed being with. Gina was beautiful, spirited, intelligent, and after three days of marriage, he couldn't imagine anyone else as his wife.

When he contemplated how easily he might have ended up with a bride he could barely tolerate, he inwardly shuddered, then thanked the fates for the spouse who complemented him in so many ways and on so many levels. He couldn't have chosen better, even if he'd tried.

"Prince Ruark," Louise interrupted his thoughts. "Because your marriage is crucial to the alliance between Avelogne and Marestonia, do you have any plans to hold a more formal ceremony in either country, with both royal families in attendance?"

Although Gina smiled as she glanced at him, he felt her squeeze his hand and saw a flash of uncertainty in her eyes.

"Not at the moment," Ruark answered smoothly.

"Would you *consider* a formal ceremony in Marestonia as a more visible show of unity?" Louise pressed. "As you know, we take pride in our royal family and it's been several years since we've enjoyed the excitement of a royal wedding."

Ruark knew he had to tread carefully. He exchanged a glance with Gina and knew she realized it, too. But while Gina didn't know where Louise's questions were headed, he did.

"Our work schedules are rather tight and we considered ourselves fortunate to marry in the manner we did." He spoke with finality, hoping Louise would accept his answer and move on.

She didn't.

"While the people of Avelogne and Marestonia understand your desire to marry here in the country where you both live and work, some might argue that sharing such a momentous occasion with your people is your duty," Louise said slyly.

"Perhaps," he conceded, "although, as a third son, I doubt if the people would expect the same pomp and ceremony required of my oldest brother."

"Perhaps not the same," she admitted, "but no matter what your place in the line of succession, you *are* a member of the royal family. More importantly, *you* are the one instrumental in resolving the current crisis. What better way to cement good relations with Avelogne than with a celebration to mark the occasion?"

What better way, indeed. Ruark exchanged another glance with Gina and saw both fear and dread in her eyes. He stroked her hand in reassurance.

"We'll take your suggestion under advisement," he said.

"Thank you, Your Highness." She turned to Gina. "It's been a pleasure meeting you, Your Highness. And best wishes for your marriage."

"Thank you," Gina murmured.

Hugh arrived at that moment to escort the two to the door. As soon as they were alone, Gina sank onto the sofa. "I do *not* want to do that again."

"You were great. She was eating out of your hand."

"Perhaps, but she was almost salivating at the prospect of a formal wedding. Frankly, if I hear the word 'duty' one more time, I think I'll scream."

Ruark smiled as he sat beside her and drew her close. "It hasn't been bad so far, has it?"

"No," she admitted. "But you're not seriously considering her suggestion, are you?"

"The possibility always existed," he admitted,

"and I'd hoped we could avoid it, but we've come too far to not see this to the end."

Her shoulders slumped. "I know. But…" Her voice faded.

"But what?"

"I just want to be a doctor," she said simply. "I want to go to work every morning and treat patients, not stand in the limelight and pretend to be something I'm not."

He understood better than she knew. He'd found it was far easier to set aside his royal trappings and focus on his profession in a country where he wasn't a household name.

"People should accept we're married without us having to go through a dog and pony show!" she continued.

"They should," he agreed. Unfortunately, as much as he wanted to tell her what she wanted to hear, he couldn't. Comforting her didn't mean giving her false hope and he respected her too much to do that. "However, Louise raised valid points. The royal family is part of the nation's identity. Treating it as something common goes against the very grain of our existence."

She fell silent. "We're going to have to do this, too, aren't we?"

"Perhaps," he prevaricated, although he wrapped his other arm around her to comfort her as best he could. "It's too soon to tell. Besides, Louise Amandine's opinions may not reflect everyone else's. Let's wait and see what happens."

Maybe there *was* a chance the highly visible ceremony wouldn't be necessary, but if Louise had broached the subject, the odds had shrunk to almost nothing. In his heart, he knew a more formal ceremony was inevitable. He wouldn't be surprised if his parents and a few trustworthy staff members had already planned the occasion from the guest list to the dinner menu.

Gina wouldn't be thrilled about this development, and the prospect bothered him. They'd married strictly for practical reasons, but he didn't want her to ever regret her decision. If making her happy served that purpose, then he would move mountains to do so.

Yet he wondered why Gina wasn't eager to go through with a royal wedding. Weren't the horse-drawn carriages, people lining the streets to wave and throw flowers, the sacredness of the cathedral, and the uniform marking his station all part of the fairy-tale ceremony that women dreamed about?

CHAPTER EIGHT

"HERE comes the happy couple!"

"Welcome back!"

Gina smiled at the staff members who greeted them as soon as she and Ruark strolled into the ER on Monday morning. Everything from the phones ringing to the familiar scent of disinfectant made her feel as if she'd finally returned to the familiar. The rest of her life had changed dramatically, but Belmont General remained her anchor.

"It's nice to know we were missed," she said.

"Of course you were," Lucy chided. "It wasn't the same without you."

"Why, thank you." Gina beamed. "It's great to be here." After being pampered like a prize poodle, she was ready for normalcy where she could fill her own coffee mug, zap her own bag of microwave popcorn, and look up a phone number without someone hovering over her.

"How was the honeymoon?" someone asked.

She glanced at Ruark, who appeared as interested in her response as everyone else, and smiled at him. "Wonderful." And it had been. Ruark had provided the one bright spot in her days.

The only bad moment had been when she'd realized their life was still not their own. After surviving an interview, the prospect of facing the fanfare associated with a royal wedding was daunting. It had been sweet of Ruark to hint that it might not be necessary, in order to spare her the worry, but her instincts told her an ostentatious ceremony couldn't be avoided. Especially after Ms Amandine had said the "D" word.

Duty.

Her father truly had bucked tradition by marrying Lizbet in a private ceremony. No doubt the people had felt robbed, and those feelings had resurfaced with a vengeance once Margret's diary had been made public.

Still, nothing was set in stone. And worrying over a possibility was a waste of energy.

"But as wonderful as it was," she continued, "I'm obviously not cut out for a life of leisure."

"Then you're in the right place," Lucy declared, "because we're expecting a trauma any minute. Car accident on the freeway." The distant sound of a siren was cut short, signaling the ambulance's approach.

"I'd say it's here," Gina remarked, already heading for the cart stacked with protective gowns and gloves as she mentally prepared for the patients who would roll through those doors.

It was definitely great to be back where she was needed.

But her sense of purpose was shaken several days later when Ruark called her into his office.

"I wanted you to be the first to know," he said as he perched on the edge of his desk. "Administration has approved my request to hire additional physicians."

"However did you manage that?" she asked, amazed. "Bill had asked for extra staff to expand our clinic services for a long time. Now we can." Seeing his sober expression, her excitement dimmed. "Can't we?"

"The extra positions aren't for the clinic. They're for the ER itself."

She studied him in puzzlement. "But we don't need more staff in the ER. I've handled—"

"Once I saw how many hours you're on duty every week—usually no less than seventy-five—

the CEO agreed we had to make a few changes. So I have."

Intuition warned her she wouldn't like the rest of this conversation. "Do I still have a job?" she asked evenly, bracing herself for his answer.

He seemed astonished by her question. "Of course. I'm simply scheduling you for a more acceptable number of hours. You can choose to work three twelve-hour or four ten-hour shifts."

She should have been relieved, even happy, by the news but she wasn't. She'd willingly worked the number of hours she had because it gave her a sense of purpose. Now he was taking it from her without warning. He may be the department's head, but he should have informed her of his plans beforehand. After all, physician coverage wasn't a topic requiring secrecy and they *were* married. That alone had to count for something, didn't it?

Frustration and pain simmered together. "When will this take effect?" she asked evenly, unable to meet his gaze because he'd surely see the hurt there.

"Next week. Until we recruit two more permanent people, we'll be using locums and they'll start on Monday. So which hours would you prefer?"

He certainly wasn't giving her any time to

mentally adjust. He'd simply snapped his fingers and it was done, but if he thought she'd thank him for his highhandedness, he could think again.

"Do I really have a choice?" This time she met his gaze, certain she'd masked her inner turmoil well enough. "Or are you going to decide for me?"

His expression was inscrutable. "I certainly could, but I'd rather not."

Gina rubbed her temple, feeling as if she was losing control of the one part of her life that she *could* control.

"This was for the good of the department, Gina," he said, as if he sensed how difficult this was for her. "On my first day here, I mentioned there would be some changes and improvements. Requiring you to cover the number of hours you did isn't in the hospital's or the patients' best interests."

Logically, she knew that, but at the moment, even though he was giving her the courtesy of a choice, she only saw the loss of the most important thing in her life.

The problem was that if she chose the three-day schedule, she'd rattle around his house, bored to tears, for four days instead of three. On the other hand, if she did choose the three day schedule, she could work elsewhere. The free clinic down the street always needed physicians.

"I might mention that your contract doesn't allow you to moonlight," he said offhandedly, as if he'd read her thoughts.

"I can donate my time," she defended.

"True, and if you choose to do that, I won't stop you."

He'd surprised her. "You won't?"

"No, but if you'd rather work round the clock instead of spend time with me, then I must be doing something wrong," he said lightly.

Now he pulled out the husband card, she thought, feeling uncharitable.

Her gut warned she was overreacting to what some might say was a thoughtful gesture on his part. Most people, especially newlyweds, would be glad to stop working sixty or more hours a week, but she wasn't "most people" or a traditional newlywed. Her career meant everything to her and had governed her life for too many years for her to lose part of it cold turkey without anything to take its place.

You have something to take its place.

Only in a technical sense, she argued. Once she

left the hospital, she had staff to handle every other detail of her life. Her career had been the one thing she'd still felt she could call her own. Now, apparently, she didn't even have that.

While she perversely wanted to take the three twelve-hour days schedule and donate her services to a clinic for the rest of the week, she enjoyed working at Belmont where the staff were like family. She refused to let Ruark take that from her, too.

"I'll take the four ten-hour shifts," she said stiffly.

The tiniest wrinkle of puzzlement appeared on his brow. "Gina, this isn't—"

"Is that all you needed?" She was proud of the cool tone in her voice. "I have patients waiting."

He clearly heard her retreat behind the defined lines of superior-subordinate. He hesitated for a fraction of second before he nodded. "There is one other thing. I heard an interesting tidbit about your former boss today."

"Bill Nevins? What's he done now?"

"He's landed a job as administrator of a fifty-bed hospital in Iowa."

"Administrator?" She was incredulous. "He's certainly moved up in the world."

"Just goes to show how some people are like

cats—no matter how they fall, they always land on their feet."

"Who would have guessed?" she mused aloud. "There truly isn't any justice in the world, is there?" Without waiting for his reply, she left.

Ruark watched her close the door before he leaned back in his chair, perplexed. Their conversation hadn't gone quite as he'd expected. She was supposed to be thrilled for the extra free time and the additional staff to lighten the workload, but instead she'd reacted as if he'd cold-bloodedly taken away her most prized possession.

Her comment, *I just want to be a doctor*, whispered in his head. Before its echo disappeared, he understood…

Although she still was and always would work in her profession if she wanted to, losing a third of her working hours clearly had made her feel as if he'd chipped away part of her career along with the rest of her life.

Yet while he regretted not preparing her for the eventuality, he had to make decisions for the good of the department. True, this particular decision would be to his personal benefit as well, but he was confident Gina would see the change as a departmental improvement rather than a personal attack. Given time, she'd see she'd gained more than she'd lost.

Gina forced herself not to fume during odd moments, but by the end of an hour she'd slowly grown to accept what she couldn't change. However, accepting the situation didn't mean she liked it.

Lucy thrust a chart into her hands. "You need to see this woman right away."

"What's wrong?"

"Severe vaginal bleeding. I've seen corpses with more color," Lucy warned.

"Did you call Stella?" Stella Fairchild was the resident house OB-GYN.

"Not yet."

"Go ahead. Meanwhile, I'll see her."

"Before you do, you should also know she's a single mom with three kids in the waiting room."

Gina went inside and found Doreen Roy lying on the bed, her color as pale as the white sheet covering her. "Hi," she said. "I'm Dr Sutton. I understand you're having a few problems."

Doreen nodded. Her light brown hair hung limply around her thin face. Lines bracketed her eyes and mouth and stretched across her forehead. The woman had clearly suffered hard times during her forty-three years.

"My periods have been getting heavier and heavier. The last few months it hasn't stopped at all. I was going to go to the doctor, but…" she picked at the hem of the sheet "…I just didn't find the time."

Money, rather than time, was probably the issue. Gina had seen cases like Doreen's more often than she cared to count. For whatever reason, the woman had chosen not to use her money on herself. After glancing at her clean but shabby clothes, and knowing three children depended on her, Gina could easily imagine where her money went.

Doreen drew a bracing breath. "I noticed my heart seems to be pounding hard and at times I can't catch my breath, but I've been managing. Then I passed out this morning while I was making breakfast for my kids. Tim, my oldest, insisted I come here. He only knows I fainted— he doesn't know about the bleeding. Some things you just don't talk about to your teenage son."

"I understand. How old is he?" Gina asked as she listened to her heart.

"Thirteen. Molly is seven and Cara is five."

"Any other symptoms you think we need to know about?" Gina asked as she studied Doreen's chart.

"Not really. I'm always cold and I sometimes have a hard time concentrating. Is that important?"

"Possibly," Gina answered. "While we're waiting for our gynecologist to perform a vaginal exam, I'm going to order a few lab tests. Then we'll decide what to do."

"Will the tests take long?"

"About an hour. Two at the most." Sensing the woman's agitation, she said kindly, "It seems like a long time, but it truly isn't."

"No, it's just that, well…I hate to leave my kids alone. I know they're worried."

"After Dr Fairchild examines you, they can wait here instead of in the waiting room. But if we need to admit you, they'll need a place to go."

"My parents are out of town until tomorrow. My neighbor would probably look after them if I asked her." Doreen closed her eyes.

Gina found Lucy in the hallway. "I want a stat CBC and tell them to call the hemoglobin ASAP, basic chemistries, coag studies, with a blood type and antibody screen. Dr Fairchild will want those results so the sooner we draw the blood samples, the better. Oh, and notify Radiology that we'll need an ultrasound."

"Will do."

"Meanwhile, I'm going to check on Mrs Roy's children."

Gina strode into the waiting area where three dark-haired children huddled together in a corner. The smallest sat on her brother's lap with her thumb in her mouth, idly twirling a lock of her shoulder-length hair as he read aloud from a dog-eared copy of *Bert and Ernie Go to the Hospital*.

"Tim?" Gina asked. "Tim Roy?"

He rose, setting his little sister on her feet. "Yes, ma'am?"

"I'm Dr Sutton and I just saw your mother."

"How is she? Is she gonna be alright?" Fear pinched his face and made him seem far older than thirteen.

"We're taking care of her," she assured him. "I've ordered several tests and as soon as we get those results, we'll have an idea of what we need to do." She eyed the trio. All were dressed in faded but clean clothes. The two girls wore matching shorts and vest tops in pink and green while Tim wore a pair of ragged denim shorts and a short-sleeved plaid cotton shirt that was not only faded but also missing two buttons. "As soon as another doctor has seen your mom, you can sit with her. Would you like that?"

The two little girls nodded, their eyes wide. The youngest had popped her thumb back into her mouth.

"It may take a while," Gina warned, "but would you like something to drink while you're waiting? Or a snack?" It was almost eleven and kids were always hungry.

"We're fine," Tim answered, almost defiantly.

"OK, but if you change your mind, soda and snack machines are around the corner."

As Gina had predicted, before the hour was up, Stella had examined Doreen Roy. The preliminary lab results had narrowed her treatment options to one.

"With her critical hemoglobin, I have to take her to surgery," the petite, dark-haired gynecologist announced as she shared the results of the ultrasound. "She's bleeding out before our eyes and until she has a hysterectomy, it won't stop."

This was exactly what Gina had suspected. "I ordered a cross-match for four units as soon as I heard her hemoglobin level. When do you want to operate?"

Stella glanced at the clock. "I can't get a suite until three, which is for the best because Mrs Roy ate this morning and I can't safely anesthetize her before then. Meanwhile, I can infuse a unit or two of blood."

Gina thought of the three children in the waiting room. "Have you broken the news yet?"

"I'd mentioned there was a good chance she would need surgery, either a D and C or a hyster-ectomy, depending on what the tests showed, but that's all."

"Unfortunately, she has three kids at home." Gina gave their names and ages. "Her parents are out of town until tomorrow."

"She can't wait until then."

"Mrs Roy mentioned a neighbor," Gina said. "I'll ask our social workers to make appropriate arrangements."

"You'd better hurry," Stella said grimly. "I can't, in good conscience, wheel her into surgery until her kids have appropriate guardianship."

"I'll tell the social workers to make this case top priority," Gina promised.

"Meanwhile, I'll talk to Mrs Roy and transfer

her upstairs to the surgical floor. Let me know if you run into a problem."

"I will," Gina promised.

After leaving a message for a social worker to visit Doreen, Gina headed for the waiting room. Before she'd gotten too far, the man she'd been trying to avoid fell into step beside her. "Can you sneak away for lunch?"

Instinctively, she stiffened, before she decided that treating him like the enemy wasn't the answer. He did what he thought he had to do, and so would she.

"Not yet," she replied. "I have three kids to see first."

"Then you'll be a while."

"Oh, they aren't sick. Their mother is having an emergency hysterectomy in a few hours and I thought they could wait with her until then." She sighed. "The problem is, she's a single mom and we're trying to sort out what to do with them until her parents return tomorrow."

"I sympathize, but what'll happen to them in the meantime?" He raised an eyebrow.

"I'm working on it."

The corner of the waiting room where she'd previously left the children was empty. "I wonder where they went," she remarked, before she heard a plaintive voice drifting around the corner where the snack machines stood.

She followed the sound and saw little Cara pressing a finger to the soda machine's clear glass window. "Can we have that, Timmy? I'm really thirsty."

"I'll take you to the water fountain," her brother answered.

"I'm hungry, too. That looks good." Cara pointed to something in the snack machine.

"I only have a dollar," he told her. "You have to pick something you can share with Molly."

Immediately, Gina tugged Ruark out of sight. "I'm taking them to lunch."

He nodded. "I had a feeling you would."

"Do you still want to join me?"

He looked surprised. "Why wouldn't I?"

"They're children. They can be messy, not to mention difficult."

His mouth twitched. "I think I can handle the stress."

Gina marched toward the trio who were debating the merits of potato chips against candies. "Hi, guys."

Tim hoisted his little sister to one hip. "How's Mom?"

"She's going to be fine," Gina told him. "But there are a few things we need to talk about. Why don't you come with me where we won't be interrupted? This is Dr Ruark Thomas, by the way."

Ruark said his hellos and shook Tim's hand and smiled at the two girls before Gina led them to a small room used for private discussions with patients' family members.

"Your mom is very sick," she said, noting how Cara sat on Tim's lap with her thumb in her mouth while Molly sat nearby, hugging an oversized bag to her chest. A scruffy brown teddy bear and a doll peeked out of the top.

"How sick?"

"She's going to need surgery. Right away."

"Is that why she fainted?"

"Yes. You see, we all have hemoglobin in our blood which carries the oxygen around our body. If our hemoglobin levels are low, we don't get enough oxygen circulating and we can pass out. Your mom's hemoglobin level is at four and it should be over twelve." She didn't mention that their mother's hemoglobin was well past the critical stage, or that if she'd waited any longer before seeking treatment, she could easily have died.

"Why is her hemoglobin so low?" he asked.

"Because she's been bleeding. Now she needs surgery to fix the problem."

"And then she'll be fine?"

"She should be."

Tim met her gaze, then Ruark's. His green eyes reflected an age far beyond his tender years. "Does she have cancer?"

"We won't know for certain until the lab runs all their tests," Gina said gently. "But let's not worry about that yet, OK?"

"Is she gonna die?" Molly asked.

"Some people who come to the hospital die," Gina explained carefully, "but a lot of people don't. They come here so we can help them get better, which is what we're going to do for your mother." She stroked the girl's hair. "OK?"

Molly nodded.

Gina rose. "The important thing right now is for you three to have lunch."

Molly's and Cara's eyes brightened. Tim frowned. "We're not hungry."

Gina suspected he was too proud to admit to the single dollar in his pocket. "Then you can keep us company while we eat. And if you should change your mind, it'll be my treat." He hesitated and she sweetened the pot. "By the time we're finished, your mom should be ready for visitors and I'll take you to her. But if you'd rather sit in the waiting room until we get back…"

Molly made a noise as she pulled on Tim's pocket to gain his attention. The silent plea she sent her brother was obvious.

He chewed on his bottom lip before he mumbled, "OK. We'll go."

Ruark hadn't seen Gina interact with children before, but from the way she treated adults, he'd expected her to be a natural with little people, too. And he was right. She handled these three like a nanny he'd once had: kind but firm enough to keep him out of mischief.

"If I hang on to the girls," she said in a voice meant for his ears only, "can you carry the food?"

After hearing her sound like his old Gina when she could still be treating him like the enemy, he would have agreed to anything. "No problem."

The girls' eyes widened at the variety spread out before them. Ruark wondered how they'd ever decide what they wanted before their lunch-hour ended, but Gina steered them toward the more kid-friendly choices.

Cara asked for a hot dog, green beans, chocolate pudding, and a side dish of olives. Molly chose macaroni and cheese, red and green gelatin squares, and fish sticks, while Tim gravitated toward the roast beef special.

Gina tossed a tuna salad sandwich on the tray for herself, along with several apples, cartons of both white and chocolate milk, and cookies. "What'll you have?" she asked. "I'm buying."

He grinned. "In that case, toss one of those chicken salad sandwiches on the tray, will you?"

After handing her lunch ticket to the cashier, she herded their group to a table. In less time than Ruark thought possible, the Roy children were wolfing down their meals as if they hadn't eaten in days. They'd certainly not enjoyed a spread like this before.

"How's the food?" he asked.

"'Licious," Cara replied as she poked a green olive on each finger and ate them one at a time.

"It's really good," Tim said as he all but licked his plate clean.

As they ate, Ruark listened as Gina chatted with their guests. In the space of thirty minutes he'd learned which schools the kids attended, what grade and which teachers they would have in the fall, their favorite subjects, how they'd spent their summer so far, and that Tim had been hired as a paper carrier three weeks ago.

Gina asked about Cara's teddy bear—his name was Buster—and Molly's doll—named Pollyanna after a book she'd read. She'd managed to draw Tim out of his shell long enough to learn his bicycle had a flat tire, and had also coaxed out important family information.

"Your mother told me your grandparents went out of town," she began.

"Grandpa took Grandma to visit her sister in Arizona," Tim answered. "They go every year."

"Grandma says this will probably be the last time, though," Molly added, "on account of Aunt Tilly has a bad heart."

"That's too bad," Gina commiserated, "but it's always nice to see people you haven't seen for a long time. Did they drive or fly?"

Tim grinned. "They drove. Grandpa said if man was supposed to fly, God would have given him wings."

The woman was wasted as a physician, Ruark decided. She should be part of a terrorist interrogation team. She could extract information without the other person knowing it.

By the end of the meal the little girls were aglow with happiness and Tim…well, the best thing Ruark could say was that Tim watched her with the same awe a normal teenage boy experienced when an attractive older woman paid him attention. His gaze followed Gina's every move and whenever she asked him a question, he would blush profusely, then stammer an answer.

Gina had three new members in her fan club, and Ruark didn't blame them a bit. Whenever he saw her, he felt as pleased, awed, and amazed as Tim did, because she was *his*.

It became far too easy to imagine her sitting at his dining room table surrounded by *their* children as she cut meat, rescued drinks from tipping over, and wheedled the day's stories out of them while making each feel important.

She was quite a woman, he thought proudly as he eyed the wide gold band he'd placed on her finger. As ridiculous as it sounded—he would never admit this to anyone—he'd be forever grateful for the furor Aunt Margret's journal had caused. All the commotion had brought Gina into his life. Doing his duty had never been this satisfying.

"What's next on the schedule?" he asked as he and Tim loaded the dirty dishes onto the cafeteria trays.

"We'll pick up a few snacks for the afternoon and then head upstairs to visit their mother. How does that sound?" she asked as she tucked the apples into Molly's bag, next to Buster and Polyanna.

"Thanks," Tim said, "but we won't need snacks, will we, kids? We'll be fine until dinnertime."

Cara frowned and Molly's smile disappeared, but they both dutifully nodded.

"If you aren't hungry, say, around three o'clock, then you can save the treats for tomorrow," Gina said, undaunted by his refusal.

"But you've already spent a lot..." Tim began.

"Friends like to do things for their friends," Gina answered firmly. "A few bags of pretzels or licorice aren't going to break my bank account. Someday, when you're grown up and have a successful career, you can do the same for someone else."

"But—"

"It's settled," Gina said, looking as determined as she sounded. "I want to do it, and that's that."

Ruark clapped his hand on Tim's shoulder. "It's easier to give in than to argue with a woman, especially this one," he told him. "She doesn't give up."

"I do not argue," she said loftily. "I merely point out the obvious."

Ruark exchanged a wink with Tim. "See what I mean?"

The boy's mouth relaxed into a soft smile. "OK, but only for the girls."

As Gina led her group to the vending machines outside the cafeteria, like a female Pied Piper, Ruark watched her purchase plenty for all three. Before long, Molly's bag was stuffed full of goodies and they trooped to the elevator that would carry them to the surgical floor.

"I'll be back in the ER as soon as I deliver them upstairs," Gina said to him. "I won't be long."

"OK." After saying his goodbyes to the children, he took the stairs and headed for his office. It hadn't been the lunch he'd planned, but it hadn't been a waste of time either. He'd seen how unselfishly she gave of herself, just like the other women in his family did. The only difference was that they'd been raised to consider the needs of others as part of their royal responsibilities while Gina did so instinctively and from her heart.

Suddenly something indefinable stirred in his chest. If he were fifteen years younger and less familiar with the games women played, he might be tempted to call it love, but he wasn't as gullible as he'd once been. He'd given up believing he'd ever experience love for himself, so that couldn't be what he was feeling.

As he considered all the things he knew and liked about her, he finally had his answer.

It was pure and utter contentment.

CHAPTER NINE

"I'M NOT going home with you tonight, Ruark," Gina announced after the shift change.

He glanced up from sliding folders into his brief-case. "Excuse me? You're not coming home?"

"I didn't say I wasn't *coming* home. I said I wasn't *going* home. At least not yet," she explained. "The social worker who'd planned to deliver the Roy children to their neighbor's house had to leave for a family emergency, so I volunteered. I'm taking my car so Hugh and Joachim will need to go with you."

After bowing to Ruark's insistence on security, their daily travel arrangements had involved Hugh accompanying Gina to work in her car with Ruark following several hours later with Joachim. At the end of the day she rode with Ruark and the two bodyguards followed.

Today, however, she'd changed the plans.

"OK," he said. "We'll follow you."

"No!" She was horrified. "I'm not taking an entire entourage to their home. I'm quite capable of finding my way. I managed to drive from point A to point B without a bodyguard all these years."

"Life is different now. There are risks."

"Yes, but—"

"I'll drive you, as always," he said firmly. "We'll *both* take the children home. And you won't know Hugh and Joachim are there."

"I didn't realize that being a princess was synonymous with being a prisoner," she accused.

"It isn't," he insisted. "But did it ever occur to you there may be factions in Avelogne and Marestonia who aren't happy about our marriage and the peace it brings? There might actually be people who *want* the two nations at each other's throats, and are looking for ways to undermine what we've done. Harming you comes to mind."

Her anger and irritation deflated. "I never imagined such a thing," she admitted.

"I'm not trying to scare you," he said, "but everyone doesn't think as we do. Some thrive on creating unrest, which is why I have to insist on appropriate security measures even though we're relatively safe living so far away. There will come a time when we won't need to be as vigilant, but it isn't today."

"You should have explained this before now," she retorted, disappointed he hadn't but finally understanding why he'd insisted on Hugh accompanying her to work each morning. She'd thought it had all been part of the pamper-the-princess routine, but she'd obviously been wrong.

"I should have," he agreed, "but you had enough adjustments to make and I didn't want to take away your peace of mind and frighten you to the point where you're looking over your shoulder all the time."

"I appreciate what you were trying to do, but it would have been easier if I'd known this from the beginning," she chided.

"I'm afraid I'm not in the habit of explaining myself," he said ruefully.

"Then you'll have to get in the habit where I'm concerned," she warned.

He smiled. "I see that. In the meantime, as far as matters of security are concerned, I'm asking you to be cautious. Don't place yourself at undue risk by venturing alone into unfamiliar territory or places where there are a lot of strangers."

Once again, she found herself accepting a situation she didn't particularly like. After freely roaming around on her own for years, being curtailed, even if for a good reason, was a difficult pill to swallow. "I won't," she promised reluctantly.

"Good." He closed his briefcase. "While you get the children, I'll tell Hugh and Joachim of our detour. Do you have the address?"

She gave it to him, hoping he wasn't familiar enough with the city to realize the Roy family lived in a rough part of town. If he did, he probably wouldn't allow her within five miles of the place.

"I won't be long," she promised, before she hurried upstairs. After allowing the children a final glimpse of their sleeping mother, who'd sailed through her surgery, she ushered them out to the parking lot where Ruark was waiting.

"Is everyone ready?" he asked as he opened the back door of his car and lifted Cara inside.

"Yes," the little girl chirped. "I been awful quiet so Mama could sleep. Dr Rock, is she supposed to sleep for a long time?"

Gina thought her mispronunciation cute and from Ruark's smile, he was amused as well. "She is," he assured her. "But when you see her tomorrow, she'll be awake."

"Good."

Gina watched Ruark buckle the two girls into the safety seats they'd borrowed from the Pediatrics Department, and as soon as Tim squeezed in beside them, they were off.

"Should we stop for dinner?" Ruark asked her in a low voice.

"The neighbor, Mrs Klimus, said she'd have dinner ready." She pointed to the next intersection. "Turn right."

While Cara and Molly chattered away in the backseat, Gina noticed Ruark's expression harden as they drove farther into the poor neighborhood. She also didn't miss how often he glanced into the rear-view mirror, as if checking on Hugh and Joachim's whereabouts.

At long last Molly cried out, "There's our street!"

Ruark made a final turn into a road that sported more potholes than flat places, then stopped in front of a weathered pink duplex bearing the number Gina had memorized. "We're here," he said cheerfully, although he cast a glance at Gina that promised retribution.

In the blink of an eye the children scampered out of the car and rushed up the cracked and uneven sidewalk.

Ruark grabbed Gina's elbow. "Do not, I repeat, do *not*, wander off," he ground out in a voice meant for her ears only.

"I won't." Although she wanted to explain that she hadn't realized this part of town had deteriorated to this extent, he plainly wasn't in the mood to listen.

Mrs Klimus, who lived on the other side of the duplex, opened the door and welcomed them in with a wide smile on her wrinkled face. She was a portly woman in her sixties and her home, although shabby, was spotless, with the aroma of something tasty drifting out of the kitchen.

"Oh, you poor, poor dears," she said as she hugged Molly and Cara. "Well, not to worry. Your mother's going to be fine." She glanced at Gina for confirmation.

"Yes, she will be," Gina answered, pleased the woman was apparently a good friend of the family. She didn't know what she would have done if they'd delivered them to a house where they weren't welcomed.

"Perfect." The woman beamed. "And don't you worry about these three either. They're practically my own grandchildren."

"I'm glad to hear it," Gina said.

"We hate to run," Ruark said smoothly, "but we have another engagement this evening."

"Of course, of course. It was delightful meeting you," Mrs Klimus said as she ushered them to the door. "Come back and visit anytime. My door is always open."

Outside, Ruark took her arm again. "Ruark, please," she protested. "I'm quite capable of walking without your help."

"I know you are, but stay behind me," he said.

She glanced at him and noticed his expression had turned grim. "What's wrong?"

"Just do as I say."

She followed his gaze and saw a young man and woman, probably in their late teens or early twenties, standing near Ruark's vehicle. Actually, the man was eyeing the vehicle and the girl was leaning against the passenger front tire as if her legs were seconds away from giving out.

As Ruark approached, the young fellow faced them. "Nice wheels," he said nonchalantly, crossing his tattooed arms over a T-shirt-clad scrawny chest before he swiped at his runny nose.

"Nice," the girl repeated in a dreamy fashion. She, too, wore low-rise jeans, but while his revealed his boxer shorts, hers revealed a pierced navel. Her eyes and lips matched the pitch-black hue of her short, spiked hair.

"Thank you," Ruark said politely as he positioned himself between the boy and Gina. "If you don't mind, we're just leaving."

"You can't go yet, man," the boy protested. "Wheels like that cost a pretty penny. You can spare a few bucks, can't you, dude?"

"Sorry, I don't carry cash," Ruark said.

"Hey, man, I'll be happy with a credit card. In fact, that sounds better."

The girl suddenly groaned, clutched her belly and slumped over. "Tony, I don't feel so good."

"A few more minutes," he promised. "Then you'll be fine."

Gina had seen enough cases in the ER to know this woman needed medical attention and soon. She was clearly coming down from her drug-induced high and if her boyfriend gave her another fix, it might well be her last.

"Your friend needs to be in the hospital," she said. "Let us call an ambulance." She reached in her pocket for her cellphone just as he whipped a long, lethal-looking knife out of his pocket.

"No. No ambulance. No cops. No doctors," he said. "Just give me your wallet and you can go."

Ruark held up his hands. "OK. Just relax and it's yours." But before he could move, Gina's own car turned the corner.

The cavalry had arrived.

Apparently realizing he'd lost his advantage because they now had witnesses, the boy flicked the knife closed, then hoisted his girlfriend onto his shoulder before he disappeared between two equally disreputable houses.

Hugh and Joachim jumped out and rushed toward them. "Are you all right, Your Highness?"

"We're fine." Ruark grabbed her arm. "Let's go."

She dug in her heels. "We can't," she protested. "That girl needs help."

Hugh walked toward the area where the two would-be thieves had disappeared. "They're long gone. We won't find them."

"Maybe we can't," she said, "but the police can. We can't just drive away and leave her. We have to do *something*."

"You heard him, Gina," Ruark reminded her. "He said no ambulance, no doctors and no cops. We can't help people who don't want it."

She shook off his grip. "Maybe, but I have to try."

He fell silent, then motioned to Hugh. While

the bodyguard punched in numbers on his cell-phone, Ruark told her, "This is pointless."

"Maybe, maybe not."

"Regardless, while we're waiting for the police, you will wait in the car."

Sensing she'd pushed him as far as she could, she obeyed. In less than ten minutes a patrol car arrived and the policemen took their statements.

"I understand your concern, Dr Sutton," the middle-aged officer, who'd clearly seen his share of sad situations, said, "but we know Tony and his girlfriend. We won't find them until they want to be found."

"And if she dies in the meantime?" she asked.

He shrugged. "There's nothing we can do short of going on a house-to-house search. I suspect Tony is already miles away. We can't search the entire city for a punk and his drugged-out girl-friend. I'm sorry, but it's a fact of life."

"Then what *can* you do?" she asked.

"We'll put out the word we're looking for her and keep our eyes open. Who knows, we may stumble across her."

Stumble across her body, she wanted to say, but she didn't. It wasn't fair to take her frustration out on the police.

"Thanks," she said. Yet as she gazed at the houses she had an overwhelming urge to knock on doors herself.

Ruark echoed her thanks before grabbing her elbow and propelling her to his car, where he all but lifted her into the backseat.

Deep in her thoughts and disappointed by her perceived failure, she hardly noticed Hugh had taken over the driver's seat. Neither did she pay much attention when Ruark turned around and began scolding her.

"This wasn't my fault," she protested mildly.

"It doesn't matter," he continued. "You went into an area that wasn't safe. You promised you would be cautious."

"I didn't know we'd be accosted," she said, staring out the window. "As for being cautious, I didn't know the neighborhood had deteriorated to the point it had, but I wasn't alone. You were with me. Hugh and Joachim were nearby."

"It wasn't safe," he insisted, as if he hadn't heard a word she'd said. "I need to be able to trust you, Gina. Trust that you'll use good judgment when I'm not with you. What if I hadn't been there? What if Hugh and Joachim hadn't arrived when they had?"

"I'd have given him my purse, as he'd asked," she said practically and evenly, because she was conscious of their audience. "And if he'd wanted the vehicle, I'd have handed him the keys, too." But it was obvious from the way Ruark ran his hands through his hair that he wasn't listening.

"And if it wasn't enough the man pulled a knife on us…" His voice rose. "You probably would have started looking for that girl on your own. Who knows what mess you would have landed in then."

His attack stung and she watched the passing scenery out of her window through tear-filled eyes. She'd said all she could in her defense; she'd show that his tirade rolled off her back instead of lodging in her heart.

Hugh pulled into their driveway and shut off the engine before he silently slipped out of the vehicle. Gina, however, didn't move.

"Well?" Ruark demanded.

"I've said all I'm going to say. I only have one question." She paused. "Are you finished?"

"For the moment," he ground out before he slid out of his seat and jerked open her door.

She strode past him without a word. Ruark followed and when she headed for the dining room, he veered toward his office. A few seconds later the door slammed.

Startled by the sound, she bumped into Hugh. "Excuse me, Your Highness," he said politely.

"It was my fault. I wasn't watching…" She stopped, hating to hear her voice tremble.

He paused and looked down at her kindly. Too kindly for her brittle nerves. It wouldn't do if she threw herself at him and sobbed on his shoulder.

"Prince Ruark doesn't usually show his temper in such a manner."

"I apparently bring out the worst in him."

"He was very worried for you. Otherwise he wouldn't have reacted so strongly to the danger."

"Your loyalty is commendable, Hugh," she said, still smarting from Ruark's wrath. "But what happened was a fluke and I won't be blamed and don't deserve to be chastised for it."

"When he calms down in a few hours, he'll understand this to be true, Your Highness."

She gave him her "yeah, right" look before she shoved aside the swinging door and entered the kitchen. Right now she needed comfort after a day full of unwelcome surprises, and a bowl of her favorite chocolate ice cream seemed perfect.

"Ice cream?" Henri was aghast as he caught her

rummaging in the freezer. "You must eat something more substantial first. How about a nice garden salad with plenty of ham and cheese?"

"Don't go to the trouble. I just want ice cream."

"It is no trouble, Your Highness," Henri fussed as he tugged the carton from her hands. "No trouble at all. Just go and sit down and I will bring it to you in a few minutes."

Foiled again! She plopped onto a dining chair and stared sullenly through the window into the back gardens. Her day couldn't have been worse. Her hours had been cut by nearly one-third, her good deed to deliver the Roy children had ended on a sour note, the young woman she'd wanted to help had disappeared, Ruark had yelled at her for something completely out of her control, and now she couldn't even eat what she wanted to!

Feeling completely adrift, she had no idea where or what her place was. Nothing was going as it should. Her husband had turned into a complete dictator after she'd actually thought she might be falling in love with him. Fat chance of that happening, because right now she didn't even *like* the man!

Give him a couple of hours to calm down, Hugh had advised. Fine. She'd give him those hours and gladly. In the meantime, she needed time alone, time to think, but she didn't want it here, in this house, where she felt like a hotel guest and couldn't do anything physical to work off her frustration.

She wanted to go home. Home, where she could eat an entire carton of ice cream without anyone gainsaying her. Home, where she could run the vacuum cleaner, dust, and mow the lawn until she was too tired to think. Home, where she'd have the breathing space to regroup before she faced the dragon again.

An overwhelming desire to escape chased away what little appetite she had. If she could only claim a short time to herself, she wouldn't waste a minute of it by eating.

"Thank you for this, Henri," she said as she carried her bowl into the kitchen, "but I'm not hungry after all. Would you please wrap it for later?"

"Of course, Your Highness."

"Oh, and I'm going out to run an errand," she lied smoothly. "I'll be back shortly."

"Would you like me to call Hugh or Joachim to accompany you?"

"No, that won't be necessary." She smiled at the Frenchman. "I'll find one of them myself."

"Very good, Your Highness."

Gina didn't waste time retrieving her purse or her spare set of car keys. Bracing herself for discovery, she was pleased to find her car still in the driveway, making it easier to slip away.

Carefully, she eased away from the house and rolled down the street, grateful her engine motor purred rather than roared. In a few short minutes she was on her way without anyone the wiser. Less than half an hour later she drove into her single-car garage and lowered the door behind her with a simple press of a button.

She was home.

As crazy as it seemed, as comforting as it was to be in familiar surroundings, she felt Ruark's absence keenly.

No, she didn't, she berated herself. She was infuriated by his utter lack of faith, his harsh words and imperious attitude. She refused to set aside her anger to remember how he'd been so kind and helpful with the Roy children at lunch, how he'd worried about her safety, how he'd positioned himself between her and danger in order to protect her.

She wouldn't dwell on the reasons for his anger because as far as she was concerned, he had none.

She'd done nothing wrong to warrant his fury. Instead, she'd concentrate on his disregard for her feelings and how he'd carelessly hurt her. Perhaps his unjustified tirade wouldn't have cut her to the quick if she didn't love him.

Oh, sweet heaven! She loved him.

Now she understood why Ruark wanted a marriage built on friendship instead of love. Love made one vulnerable, especially if it was one-sided. The only question now was, what did she do next?

Every emotion she felt tumbled and swirled together until her chest ached. Before could slide out from behind the steering-wheel and enter her safe haven, she burst into tears.

Ruark left his office some hours later, determined to find Gina and apologize for losing control. He should have trusted his instincts once they'd gotten within a few blocks of the Roy family duplex, called Hugh to stick right on their tail, and waited until his two men arrived before they'd gotten out of the vehicle. But he hadn't, and he'd taken his anger with himself out on her.

He strolled through the house, poking his nose in nearly room looking for her. When he didn't find her he headed for the backyard, certain she'd decided to watch the sunset.

Returning inside, he ran into Hugh. "Have you seen Gina?"

"Not since we arrived, sir," the bodyguard answered.

"I wonder where she is," Ruark mused aloud as a frisson of fear began to wiggle a path down his spine.

"Ah, you're back, Hugh," Henri said as he bustled past. "Did the princess say if she'd like a snack? She wasn't hungry earlier."

"Back?" Hugh frowned. "I never left."

The smile on Henri's cherubic face disappeared. "But…the princess said she had an errand to run. I offered to summon you, but she said she would find you herself." His expression cleared. "She must have taken Joachim."

"He's been here all evening," Hugh said, exchanging a glance with Ruark before hurrying away.

"I don't understand." Concern etched the chef's face as he looked at Ruark.

"Gina is missing," he said grimly.

Hugh returned, breathless. "Her car is gone."

Ruark said two words. "Find her."

Moments later, in Hugh and Joachim's office,

which was the base of their security operations, Ruark studied the monitors, which were fed by the surveillance cameras. With other security measures in place, he hadn't insisted on anyone constantly watching the footage, but maybe it was time he did. She would have been stopped within moments, although it would have only reinforced her opinion that she was a prisoner.

"I can't believe she left," he muttered, but in his heart he wasn't surprised.

"Pardon me for saying so, Your Highness," Hugh said carefully as he typed commands on his keyboard, "but you were rather hard on her."

"Thanks for stating the obvious," he snapped. "The question is, where did she go?" He turned to the man who'd seen her last. "Henri?"

He shrugged. "She mentioned an errand. I did not presume to ask what it was."

Joachim accessed the latest surveillance tape of the property and located the footage taken several hours earlier. Sure enough, Gina had climbed into her car and driven away. Ruark took comfort that she only carried her purse and not a suitcase. But where could she have gone?

"Call Belmont," he ordered. "She may be visiting a Mrs Roy on the second-floor surgical unit."

"I don't think so, sir." Hugh accessed another screen on his computer. "The GPS co-ordinates aren't near the hospital. If you'll permit me a few minutes, I can tell you exactly where she is. Or rather where her car is. We are fortunate we took the liberty of installing a GPS receiver in her vehicle when we installed a security system at her home."

Deciding to reward the man later for his foresight, Ruark leaned over Hugh's shoulder for a closer view. "And?" he demanded, impatient for the answer.

The screen zoomed in to reveal the electronic map markings. "The princess is at her old residence."

Ruark bowed his head in relief.

An unfamiliar noise startled Gina out of her deep sleep. So much for her plan to return to Ruark's house before he noticed she'd slipped away from her watchdogs, she thought tiredly. By the time she drove back, he'd be ready to deliver another scathing lecture.

"You're awake." His voice drifted across the room.

She bolted upright. "Ruark! What are...? How did...? I locked the door," she said, brushing at the trails of dried tears on her face. "I know I did so you can't accuse me of being careless."

"You did," he agreed. "Thanks to modern technology, once I realized you were missing, we were able to locate you. As for the door, the lock wasn't a problem." He held up a keyring and jingled it. "Why did you leave?"

She stared at him, incredulous. "Do you have to ask?"

"No, but I'd like to hear your reasons anyway."

"I had to get away," she said stiffly. Then, after deciding to move the inevitable confrontation out of the bedroom, she headed for the living room. "If you're going to yell, get it over with."

"I won't yell."

He'd surprised her, but as she glanced at his face, the coldness she'd seen earlier had disappeared. He almost seemed…contrite, but that wasn't possible. "Then what are you doing here?"

"I wanted to be sure you were all right. I was worried," he said simply. "For the second time today, I might add."

"As you can see, I'm fine." She glanced at the clock. "I hadn't planned to stay this long, but I fell asleep. We can go now."

He shook his head and sat on the sofa. "Not until

you explain why you left. If you wanted privacy, there were any number of rooms you could have used. You didn't have to drive across town."

The dam inside her broke and she let loose all the things preying on her mind. "*You* wanted privacy, Ruark, but I wanted something more. I left because I needed a place where I could think and be myself. Where life was *normal*. It isn't *normal* at your house. It might be for you, but it isn't for me. The staff treats me like a guest. And you..." She swallowed hard to clear the sudden lump in her throat. "Today you treated me like a useless, brainless ornament, a stupid, naïve child.

"Here, in my house, I'm me. Gina Sutton. The adult who cleans up her own messes, cooks her own meals, eats ice cream whenever she wants, decides and is accountable for her own actions. And here no one yells at me.

"At your mansion, I don't know who I am, other than a person who's created more work and more worry for everyone. Including you."

He fell silent. "What can I do to make it better?"

"Oh, no," she protested, shaking her head. "Don't you dare be gallant or kind or understanding when a few hours ago..." The words caught in her throat and she blinked rapidly. She'd cried all the tears she intended to cry.

"A few hours ago I acted like a horse's ass," he said bluntly. "I was angry with myself and I took it out on you."

His admission took her by surprise. "Angry with yourself? Why? You weren't responsible for what happened any more than I was."

"I didn't listen to my instincts and as a result you were this close…" he pinched his forefinger and thumb together "…to getting hurt. It was unforgivable to put a woman I'd sworn to honor and protect at risk. I felt as if I'd failed you."

As her proud husband humbled himself, her anger melted into forgiveness. She sank beside him and rested one hand over his.

"You can't plan for every eventuality or protect me from every possible danger," she said softly. "It's sweet of you to try, but you can't predict what will happen and you can't feel guilty if something does. It isn't healthy for either of us."

"I'd rather be too cautious than not cautious enough."

"There has to be a happy medium and it'll take time to find it. Meanwhile, you can't surround me in bubble wrap."

"Maybe not, but you can't disappear like you did either."

"You said to avoid places with strangers and unfamiliar territory," she pointed out. "My house didn't apply."

He raised an imperious eyebrow.

"Next time, I'll tell someone my exact destination," she promised on a long-suffering note, certain there would be instances when she'd chafe at the restriction. "But once you knew where I was, did you really need to check on me? Or did you think I wouldn't go home on my own?"

"You're my wife," he said simply, as if that was all the excuse he needed. "I felt certain you were safe and knew you'd return eventually when tempers cooled, but being here meant I could talk you into coming home sooner rather than later."

"Hmmm." She pretended to consider her options as she ran her finger down the placket of his shirt. "If you take time to persuade me, we won't get home until later. But if you'd rather leave sooner…" She nudged a button out of its hole.

He stilled her hand, then shot to his feet as he pulled her with him. "We'll go later," he said as he led her to the bedroom. "Much later."

CHAPTER TEN

GINA twisted her charm bracelet as she stood at the ballroom entrance on Friday night and surveyed the crowd already assembled. Other than Ruark, she didn't know a soul, although she recognized several guests because she watched television and read newspapers. Her father may have been a prince, but she wasn't accustomed to rubbing elbows with the rich and famous. In spite of her ancestry, she was merely a staff physician at a struggling hospital in a mid- to low-income neighborhood.

As she glanced at the man beside her—the man who was too handsome for words in his black tuxedo—she realized she was wrong. She wasn't only a physician. She was the Prince of Marestonia's wife, a princess, a countess in her own right. This may be her first fancy charity ball, but she belonged there as much as anyone else did.

Yet she couldn't deny she felt more at home in

her ER, wearing scrub suits and tennis shoes instead of gorgeous gowns and jewelry.

Ruark took her hand and threaded it through his. "You're fidgeting." He'd leaned over to speak in her ear, appearing as if he'd uttered an endearment rather than a gentle rebuke.

"Sorry," she whispered back. "Can't help it."

"Try."

"But everyone's staring."

"They always do when a beautiful, poised woman makes an entrance."

Having checked herself in the mirror before they'd left, she couldn't deny she looked fantastic. The hairdresser had worked wonders, an expert had applied her makeup, and her simple white evening gown glittered under the crystal chandeliers. As Ruark had mentioned he would, he'd helped her settle on her mother's single strand of pearls and matching earrings.

As for being poised, if she hadn't had Ruark's supporting arm, she'd probably have fallen off her high heels.

"This is quite awesome," she said, noting everything from uniformed waiters and fresh flowers in abundance to elaborate ice sculptures and champagne fountains. "Very glitzy and glamorous."

He glanced across the way, studying the scene as if he were seeing it for the first time. "It is," he agreed.

"I hope the women's shelter project receives a ton of money tonight. Every time a battered woman comes into the ER, I have this overwhelming urge to hunt down the man responsible and give him a dose of his own medicine!"

"I had no idea I'd married such a Valkyrie," he said with a smile. "You'll be pleased to know that women and children's causes are dear to my mother's heart as well."

He motioned ahead. "I see a few people we have to greet. Shall we?"

This was it. "Lead on."

Ruark guided her into the throng where he introduced her to the host of the ball and his wife, then the Marestonian ambassador.

The distinguished white-haired man kissed her hand as he bowed. "Your Highness. What a supreme pleasure to meet you."

She blushed. "Thank you, Ambassador Janssen."

He turned to Ruark with a twinkle in his eye. "Now I understand the rumors of a whirlwind romance. But they were not just rumors, were they, for you to land such a lovely bride?"

Ruark laughed. "One must do whatever is necessary to eliminate any and all competition when such a prize is at stake."

"You have done the royal house and your country proud."

"Thank you."

"The two of you must come to Marestonia soon for a wedding trip. The people are eager to welcome the two of you and will feel slighted should you delay."

Ruark bowed ever so slightly. "As soon as we're able to rearrange our schedules."

Apparently satisfied by Ruark's response, the ambassador moved away.

"I had no idea there was a Marestonian embassy in the vicinity," she said, "much less that an ambassador of your country would attend a ball for a national cause."

"There isn't," he admitted. "However, several of the organizers of this event have ties to Marestonia and Avelogne. As word got out that we were attending, the guest list grew to include more of our countrymen from across the US. You, my dear, were the draw card. I suspect the charity will do quite well as a result."

"Oh, my." The news only increased the pressure

she was under to present Ruark and herself in a good light.

"For the record, you dazzled the ambassador."

"Really? How could you tell?"

"A man knows these things," he replied.

"Dazzled or not, was he politely telling us the natives are restless and you need to hurry home?"

"*We*," he corrected her. "*We* need to hurry home, but that's a worry for another day. Would you like to dance?"

She grinned. "I thought you'd never ask. Just don't try anything fancier than a waltz."

"One waltz, coming up."

The next few hours were like living out a fairy tale. The musicians were exceptional, the food mouthwateringly delicious, and the company beyond compare. Having the man she loved at her side made everything else fade into the background.

Gina danced with Ruark as well as several of his compatriots. She met senators and cabinet members, CEOs of several Fortune 500 companies, and several other ambassadors, including Ambassador Antoine Lauwers of Avelogne.

"Prince Ruark," he said as he took Gina's hand and beamed at her, "I congratulate you on finding Prince Arthur's gem."

Ruark smiled. "Thank you."

"May I once again extend the Queen Mother's and King Henrik's invitation to visit Avelogne. Both the royal family and the people of Avelogne would be thrilled to honor the Princess Gina and her husband."

Gina paraphrased Ruark's earlier response. "Should we find ourselves able to rearrange our schedules, we'll consider the invitation."

The ambassador meandered away as an old friend of Ruark's joined their group. After Ruark had introduced her to Jason Dumont, a man he'd known since primary school, Gina excused herself for a trip to the punch bowl. There, she simply watched the guests, wishing she could bottle this moment and share it with Cara and Molly. She easily imagined those two little girls staring at this scene in wide-eyed wonderment.

Thank goodness things had turned out so well for their family. She shuddered to think of how different the situation could have been if friends like Mrs Klimus and relatives hadn't been on the scene.

As she glanced over at her husband and saw him laugh and joke with Jason, she wondered if he missed *his* family, friends, and the culture he'd grown up with. Probably no more than his family missed him. Even with the telephone and Internet, his mother probably hated having an ocean separate them.

Had her grandmother missed her father after he'd moved here and started his new life? No doubt she'd taken his decision to relinquish his claim to the throne as a personal rejection. For the first time she felt the heartache that her grandmother must have suffered because of one poor, misguided woman.

Perhaps it *was* time to accept the olive branch her father's family had extended. It would have been so nice after he'd died to have had the support system the Roy children now enjoyed. Maybe it wasn't too late after all…

But before she would rectify that situation, she had to do something that was far more personal. She had to find a way to tell Ruark she loved him. She could only hope that the care and concern he'd shown for her these past few weeks meant that his cynical views had softened and that love had grown in his heart, as it had in hers.

Jason clapped Ruark on the shoulder. "You always did have remarkable taste in women but you've outdone yourself, my friend. She is a treasure beyond compare and all I can say is you're a lucky dog."

Ruark grinned, delighted by his old school chum's approval. "I am, aren't I?"

"Are you certain she doesn't have a sister hidden away?"

Ruark chuckled at his hopeful tone. "I'm positive."

"She's definitely one of a kind. No wonder you snapped her up without giving us a clue you were in a relationship. When did you two meet and how in the world did you keep your romance a secret?"

"We both attended a medical seminar in California some months ago." Ruark glossed over the details, purposely avoiding any reference to how he'd conducted his supposed romance. "And the rest, as they say, is history."

"Yeah, you've definitely made history," Jason remarked. "I'd heard rumblings of how the problems between Avelogne and Marestonia prompted your marriage, but after seeing you two tonight, anyone with one eye and half a brain would know the gossip isn't true."

Ruark wasn't surprised by the rumors—they'd been bound to surface. However, Jason's observations had piqued his interest and he hoped his friend would elaborate. "Oh?"

"Yeah." Jason grinned. "I noticed as soon as I saw you across the room. You look at your wife as if you can't bear to let her out of your sight. You obviously love her."

Love her? Impossible. He cared about her and appreciated her, but that was all. Unfortunately, he couldn't disagree. Some confidences couldn't be shared even with old friends. If people thought him in love with his wife, then he'd accomplished his mission.

"I have to say," Jason continued, "after your experience with that actress, I never expected you to tie the knot."

"Neither did I," Ruark agreed, because it was true. Had duty not come into play, he'd still be a bachelor. Regardless of how Jason interpreted what he'd seen, he might not love his wife, but he was happy with his marriage.

Contented with the thought, he caught a glimpse of Gina as the crowd parted. She'd been remarkable this evening and had charmed everyone she'd met, as he'd known she would. With her tawny-colored hair and brilliant green eyes, she was a vision in her iridescent white gown, and she was his. He met her gaze and smiled.

Jason reached out and grabbed a bottle of imported beer from a passing waiter. "I'd stay and chat, but I have my eye on a gorgeous redhead and she looks like she's lonely. Give my regards to your wife and if you ever need a godfather, I'm available." He winked as he saluted Ruark, then disappeared into the throng seconds before Gina rejoined him.

"Where did Jason go?" she asked.

"Hunting," he replied. At her puzzled frown, he explained. "For a redhead."

"Ah."

"Is Cinderella ready to leave her first ball, or would she like to stay longer?"

"It's well past midnight," she pointed out. "If we won't commit some horrible breach of etiquette, I'd like to go. As much as I've enjoyed myself, I wouldn't mind slipping out of the spotlight."

"Then we'll go." He was more than eager to cut the evening short. Sharing Gina with so many people had begun to fray his patience. Not only that, but he had a special day planned for tomorrow—today, actually—and he didn't want anything to mar his surprise.

* * *

"Wake up, sleepyhead."

Gina groaned at the sound of Ruark's voice. He sounded entirely too chipper for…she glanced at the clock with one eye…9:00 a.m. He was obviously used to functioning on less sleep than she was because they hadn't gotten home until after two.

Closing both eyes, she stretched. "What's the rush? It's Saturday."

"Exactly. We have places to go, things to do."

Suddenly a T-shirt and a pair of shorts landed on her face, and startled her completely awake. "What?"

Ruark stood above her and grinned, wearing a disreputable pair of jeans and faded cotton shirt. "Come on. We're wasting time. Everyone's waiting. We can't get started until you get up."

A quiet knock at the door summoned him. He returned with a steaming mug of coffee and placed it on the nightstand. "Henri sent this. You have five minutes or you're coming with me in your pj's."

She jumped out of bed at his threat. "What's going on?"

"You'll see," he said cryptically.

Gina dashed into the bathroom to rush through her morning routine and exchange her nightgown for the clothes Ruark had so graciously chosen for her. She was halfway down the stairs when he met her in the foyer.

"What's going on?" she asked.

"It's moving day," he said.

She stopped short. "Moving? We're moving?"

"Not in the sense you're thinking." He escorted her to the game room, which was a few doors down from his office. Inside, she saw Hugh, Joachim, and Henri dismantling the slate pool table.

"You're moving the pool table?" she asked, wondering why he'd insisted on her presence.

He nodded. "Remember how you said you didn't have a place to call your own? Now you have one. This will be *your* room to organize and use as you see fit."

Gina took in the cathedral ceiling, the window overlooking the flowerbeds in the backyard, the beautiful oak hardwood floor. "It's mine?" she asked, hardly able to believe he was giving up one of his masculine domains for her.

"All yours. As soon as we clear out what you don't want, we can either bring in furniture from your other house or purchase new."

"But your game room," she protested.

"We aren't doing away with it entirely," he said.

"We're only relocating it to the empty area over the garage."

Touched by his gesture, she was momentarily speechless. "Oh, Ruark. I don't know what to say. I'm completely overwhelmed. This is so sweet of you."

He grinned, looking remarkably boyish. "Overwhelmed or not, we're operating on a time schedule here. We have to turn the moving van back to the rental company by 8:00 p.m. so before we can cart anything in, this room has to be emptied out."

"Wouldn't it be easier if I took the space over the garage?"

"Not only would you be too far away from the rest of the house but it's an inappropriate location for my wife to receive guests. This," he emphasized, "is your room."

Thinking of some of the women she'd met last night, she realized he was right. "OK. I'll keep the cabinet and the small table. The rest can go. Including the mounted antlers and the bearskin rug."

"Are you sure? Antlers and a bearskin rug are great conversation starters," Ruark teased.

"Then you might want them in *your* office."

"You heard her, guys. We're hauling them upstairs."

With much groaning and moaning, the four men heaved the furniture to its new home. The pieces of slate were the most difficult to maneuver. When Ruark's corner slipped and slammed into his shoulder, nearly knocking him off his feet and down the steps, Gina's heart leaped into her throat.

"This isn't a good idea," she warned. "We should have waited for a crew of experienced movers."

"Don't be ridiculous," Ruark huffed as soon as they reached the top and unceremoniously dropped their load. "This isn't any worse than lifting weights at the gym."

Hugh and Joachim wiped sweaty foreheads with their arms, looking as alarmed as she felt at Ruark's close call with disaster. "Your Highness," Hugh began, "perhaps we should consider recruiting a few more hands for the job?"

"The heaviest piece—the pool table—is done. We can handle the rest."

Gina didn't know if Ruark was determined to show off or simply too stubborn to admit defeat, but she added her muscles to the mix. Before long, the room's contents had been transferred and they were on their way to her old house.

There, she selected several of her favorite pieces, including a roll-top desk, sofa and chairs, an heirloom cedar chest and an elaborately hand-carved wardrobe that had belonged to her parents. She also boxed her frog collection, determined to place the ceramic frog wearing a jaunty expression and a crown on his head in a prominent place because it reminded her of Ruark.

By five o'clock that evening, other than a fresh coat of paint and new window treatments, the Princess's Room, as Henri had dubbed it, was ready.

"I can't thank you all enough," Gina said as she hugged each tired helper to their sheepish embarrassment. "You are all the best."

"We were pleased to do this for you," Hugh said before the three of them disappeared, leaving Gina alone with Ruark.

"They didn't have to rush off," she said, surprised by how quickly they'd left.

"They probably thought they should go before you asked them to rearrange the furniture again," he said dryly.

"I did work them rather hard," she admitted.

"And what about your poor husband?" he asked.

She slipped her arms around his neck. "He was sorely used, too. I'll have to make it up to him."

He groaned as she squeezed. "I believe every muscle in my body aches."

"Why don't you soak in the Jacuzzi for a while? I'll bring a snack to tide us over until Henri calls us to dinner."

"An excellent suggestion," he said, planting a swift kiss on her mouth before they parted company.

Fifteen minutes later, she found him in the master bathroom's whirlpool tub, eyes closed. "How's the water?" she asked as she placed her tray of cheese and fresh fruit on the ledge.

"Great. Care to join me?"

"Maybe later. You need to recharge your batteries first."

As he opened his mouth to protest, she popped in a cube of Cheddar cheese and noticed the purpling bruise on his shoulder.

"You *did* hurt yourself," she accused, hating to think he'd injured himself because of her. If she hadn't loved him before, his actions today would have tipped the balance.

"It's nothing. What else did you bring?" he asked, peering at the tray.

She speared a chunk of pineapple and fed it to

him. "Fruit. I chose all of your favorites, so lie back and enjoy."

He leaned back in the whirlpool. "I could get used to this," he said as she offered a grape this time. "We could make this a nightly event."

She chuckled. "Annually."

"Weekly," he countered.

"Monthly."

"Sold."

While they devoured the food she'd brought, they talked of inconsequential things, but Gina knew in her heart that the moment she'd been waiting for, the moment when she opened herself up and revealed her feelings, was fast approaching.

"Last bite," she said as she placed a grape in his mouth.

He grabbed her free arm. "I'm still hungry."

"I'll see if Henri—"

"Not for food," he said as he tugged her shirt upwards. "For you."

She grinned. "But I'm out here and you're in there."

"A problem easily rectified. Join me."

"We can't both fit."

"Trust me. We can and we will."

She didn't hesitate. Her clothes disappeared in short order, discarded in an untidy heap near the tub.

The water was warm and only added to the sensual spell. He positioned her in front of him, between his legs, and she leaned against his chest, enjoying the feel of his muscles against her back. He began soaping her skin as his mouth trailed kisses down the side of her neck. He gently caressed, stroked, and teased every nerve ending of her entire body until she was certain they'd raised the temperature of the water swirling around them.

They might have been there for minutes or hours, she didn't know because she was too caught up in his tender assault of her senses. Finally, he rose with a growl, wrapped a towel around her and himself, then carried her to their bed.

Eager for him, she gratefully accepted his weight as he covered her completely. The ache inside her demanded ease and she dug her fingers into his back as he nuzzled her neck.

"Ruark, please," she murmured.

"Please what?"

"Please…hurry."

With one touch he sent her to the stars. With one smooth thrust he filled her, then began a fierce rhythm that didn't end until he groaned and collapsed against her.

Gina drifted back to earth, her arms and legs intertwined with his as she rested her cheek against his chest and listened to his steady heartbeat. Her scattered thoughts slowly coalesced into one that summed up everything in her heart.

"I love you," she confessed softly as her fingertips traced swirls on his chest.

His grip around her tightened. "I told you we'd be good together."

She heard the pride, the self-satisfaction in his voice. "Pretty sure of yourself, weren't you?"

"You bet."

"And you based this on…?"

"Sixth sense. Intuition. Gut feeling."

Certain she'd taken him by surprise with her declaration of love, she pressed on. "Does your sixth sense tell you anything else besides we're good together?"

He hesitated. "Is it supposed to?"

The excitement of saying she loved him dimmed, but perhaps he simply needed coaxing. "After all this time, I thought maybe our relationship had grown past the we-get-along-great stage."

She sensed his mental withdrawal. "Is that what

you want from me?" he asked. "To tell you what you want to hear? To say I love you?"

Hardness had replaced the lazy quality of his voice and she winced at the sudden loss of their closeness. "Only if you mean it," she said.

He rolled off her to sit up on the edge of the bed, his bare back toward her. "We've talked about this concept of love before. You entered into this marriage knowing it was to fulfill a duty, knowing we would build a relationship based on respect and mutual interests, rather than feelings."

"I know what I agreed to," she said. "But my feelings changed."

"Exactly my point. Emotions shift as easily as the tide. Today you say you love me—who knows what you'll feel tomorrow?"

She pulled the sheet around her, suddenly uncomfortable at baring her body as well as her soul. "My feelings didn't just change, Ruark. They *grew*. They'll be the same tomorrow as they are today."

He turned to face her, his expression disbelieving. "What if I suddenly refuse to grant your every whim? To give you the things that you like and enjoy? What then?"

A disquieting thought rushed forward in her mind. "Is that what you've been doing, Ruark?" she asked quietly. "Was today just one more instance of you acting like a benevolent genie? Did you really want a happy marriage, or did you only want the *illusion* of one?"

"I didn't want an illusion," he insisted. "As far as I'm concerned, our marriage is everything we'd expected and tried to make it. Five minutes ago we proved how good it is."

She released the breath she hadn't realized she'd been holding. For a minute there she'd been afraid he'd only been deceiving her, using her as a pleasant perk associated with performing his duty.

"Happiness is a feeling," she pointed out. "But love is stronger because it grows, which is what happened to me. As I got to know you, I fell in love." She paused. "I'd hoped you'd had the same experience."

He turned to face her. "I do care about you," he said soberly. "Why can't that be enough?"

"Because it isn't," she said, saddened that he'd still closed his heart off to her in spite of everything they shared. "Love makes the day seem brighter, problems less insurmountable, life more enjoyable. Without it, you're not really living, only going through the motions."

"Love is simply a word. Nothing more, nothing less."

She rose as regally as possible and twisted the sheet toga-style around herself. "You loved a woman once—"

"I was wrong," he said.

She ignored his interruption. "And she told you what she wanted you to hear. I'm not her, though, so don't transplant her flaws onto me. I have enough of my own.

"I know she left you, but I won't," she stated, knowing that was part of his concern. "Not because I can't give up the princess lifestyle but because I made a promise which I intend to keep. Our marriage can either be heaven or hell. The choice is yours."

She swept from the room and locked herself in the master bathroom. The need to weep swept over her, but she gritted her teeth and held back the sob. Instead, she splashed water on her face and patted her skin dry, wishing she could wash away the pain of his rejection as easily.

He *didn't* love her. Maybe his caring was simply a way to make the performance of his duty more palatable. She couldn't deny they were compatible in many areas, but she didn't want to be his consolation prize, the reward granted to a good obedient little prince for services rendered to the Crown.

For a moment she felt trapped in a loveless marriage, but as she remembered all the things he'd done to ease her into her new life, all the ways he'd made her feel special, she couldn't—*wouldn't*—believe that he didn't feel something beyond companionship. Yesterday he'd worried about failing her, and he wouldn't have done that if she wasn't important to him. He simply couldn't admit that his caring was love in disguise.

Considering all his experiences with women who'd pretended to care because he was a prince, she was fortunate he cared at all. He could so easily have held himself back and turned their relationship into a case of "married singles".

Maybe that was the problem, she thought as hope edged away her sense of entrapment. He was afraid to believe her, afraid to *let* himself love her. Married or not, they'd only known each other for a few weeks and he obviously didn't trust her yet with something as important as his heart. She'd simply have to prove that her declaration hadn't been as a result of her hormones or gratitude for his generosity. That she'd fallen in love with the man, not his title.

It would take patience and effort to smash through his walls of skepticism, she consoled herself. He'd spent years building his defenses, so she couldn't expect to tear them down on her very first try. She'd inherited enough of her father's stubbornness to keep swinging and stay in the game.

She would show him that love, not companionship or mutual interests, made a marriage happy. Teach him that love meant strength, not weakness or vulnerability.

If he didn't learn the lesson? What then?

She didn't know, she thought miserably, but the picture of her life if she failed was too bleak and too miserable to contemplate.

Ruark jerked on clean clothes, irritated at how easily the afternoon had turned from pure bliss into sheer agony. Gina had known from the beginning that he didn't want or expect love to be a part of their marriage and suddenly, because he'd done a few nice things, she went and changed the rules.

Well, he wouldn't have it. The foundation for their relationship had been set. Trust, companionship, respect, and attraction had been part of the package. He hadn't planned to invest himself emotionally in their arrangement and she shouldn't have either.

Oh, he truly cared about her, more than any other woman he'd spent time with, and that should have satisfied her. Why did she want words that were often uttered carelessly or with deceit? Didn't she know that they only gave false hope and made one vulnerable?

As far as he was concerned, actions spoke louder and more honestly than words ever could. Gina would simply have to accept and be contented by that.

CHAPTER ELEVEN

"HAVE you seen the latest *People* magazine?" Lucy asked Gina a week later.

Gina sighed. Ever since photos of the women's shelter project charity ball had hit the tabloids, her excited staff had gone out of their way to hunt down every bit of publicity about the royal couple they could. At first, it had been sweet, but now she found it irritating, especially as her grand plan seemed to be failing.

She'd done her best to act as she always had, with one exception. Now, every chance she got, she told Ruark both in word and deed that she loved him. Unfortunately, he wasn't replying in kind, and she'd given him ample opportunity.

A relationship expert on the Internet had claimed that men who couldn't say they loved someone had commitment issues. As marriage was a huge commitment which they'd already undertaken, she discarded the theory soon after she'd read it. She was simply expecting too much, too soon, but her continued failure was disheartening.

If only he hadn't been so darned sweet during the past week!

First, he'd ventured into the kitchen and mixed a batch of her favorite double chocolate peanut butter chip cookies with Henri's help. The only way he could have known she enjoyed them so much was if he'd noticed she always added them to her lunch tray.

Then he'd sent her a basket of tiger lilies, admitting he'd known how much she enjoyed them. How he'd learned they were her favorite, she couldn't begin to guess because none of her friends knew just how special those flowers were. Her father would send them on special occasions or whenever she'd had a really tough week at school. She'd deck her parents' graves with them every year on their birthdays and Memorial Day, and whenever she felt especially blue, she bought them for herself.

As for her nights with Ruark, they were as fantastic as always. She would always tell him she loved him, but she'd stay awake long after he did, hoping to hear a whispered endearment before he fell asleep. Unfortunately, she never did.

For the first time in her career she almost

wished she'd studied psychology instead of emergency medicine.

"Hello?" Lucy asked. "Anybody home?"

Gina focused on the nurse. "Sorry. Don't mind me. My mind was…elsewhere."

"Can't imagine why," Lucy said cheerfully. "Want to hear what they said about you in *Home and Garden*?"

"No."

"Too bad. It's quite flattering." She closed the magazine and laid it on the stack of other publications that contained some mention of the royal couple.

"I don't know why you guys are collecting all this," Gina said, wishing she could make the pile vanish and knowing she'd cause an outcry if she did. "The entire department sees us almost every day. You don't need photos."

"Hey, these are for posterity," Lucy protested. "You're the closest we'll ever come to knowing a celebrity so we're milking it for all its worth. We get so little enjoyment out of life here in the trenches."

"Yeah, right. Speaking of trenches, do we have the lab work back on room four?" At Lucy's blank look, Gina pointed to the scheduling board. "Does chest pain ring a bell?"

"Oh, yeah, him. I've been busy with the guy whose nail gun misfired and shot a nail into his hand. Before you ask, Dr Holman is making arrangements to admit him for surgery."

Owen Holman was a top-notch orthopedic surgeon who specialized in hand injuries. "Great. But what about—?"

"The lab work isn't back yet. I checked the printer a few minutes ago. My bet's on indigestion."

"Hold onto your money," Gina advised. "He could fool you. What else do we have?"

"Nothing our PA can't handle. Before I forget, Dr Thomas wants to see you. Preferably before his meeting with Dr Lansing at ten."

Frankly, she'd like some distance from the man until she sorted through her troublesome thoughts, but apparently she wouldn't get any. "OK, but the minute those lab results come through, I want to see them."

"Will do. Oh, and, Gina?"

She turned and faced the nurse. "Yes?"

"You've seemed rather preoccupied today." Lucy's face registered concern. "Is everything OK?"

"Sure. Why wouldn't it be?"

The nurse shrugged. "You seem different.

More…restrained, I suppose. Are you feeling well?"

"I'm fine. Truly," she replied, as much to assure Lucy as herself. "And remember, I'm waiting for those results."

As directed, Gina went to Ruark's office. His desk was covered in what she knew were budget proposals and cost analyses, but he was leaning back in his chair, reading a magazine article.

She groaned as she rubbed the back of her neck in abject frustration. "Not you, too."

He grinned sheepishly as he straightened. "Couldn't resist. According to this, ever since we announced our wedding, the incidents of vandalism and other property crimes have dropped significantly. People are speculating on the details and what long-term effects our marriage will have on the two countries. It's obvious the mood in Avelogne and Marestonia has improved."

Just what she needed—to be reminded of why they'd gotten married. "I'm glad," she said simply. "Is that why you wanted to see me?"

He closed the magazine and tossed it onto his desk. "No." He studied her. "Are you OK?"

Irritated that he was the second person to ask the

same question, she ground her teeth together before she evened her tone. "I'm fine. I'm swamped outside, and all this press is getting to me."

"The novelty will wear off soon."

"I hope so."

"As you're busy, I won't keep you, but my father called a few minutes ago. Apparently, in spite of the good news I just told you, the royal family is under pressure for us to have an official state wedding ceremony."

The idea struck fear into her heart. Although part of her had anticipated the possibility, when the subject hadn't resurfaced since the charity ball, she'd hoped it wouldn't.

"Do we have to?" she asked. "I mean, will we start an uprising if we don't?"

"No, but as I've been living in the US for some time, he's afraid the people will believe I'm dismissing my heritage if I don't honor our royal traditions."

"I see." In other words, his duty hadn't ended yet and, if the truth be known, never would. "What would be involved?" she asked, certain she wouldn't like her options.

"Our ceremony won't be as elaborate as my brother's," he assured her. "A trip down the main thoroughfare in a horse-drawn carriage, I would guess, then on to St Gregory's Cathedral for the formal church blessing. After that, we'll greet the public at the palace and host a small reception for family and friends."

Her breath caught at his mention of the church. "What did you tell him?" she asked.

"Only that I'd discuss it with you."

It had been difficult enough to marry a man who didn't love her the first time, but to repeat the experience? And in such a holy setting? Hardly. She had her limits as to what she was willing to do to right past mistakes.

"Did he indicate when this happy event is supposed to occur?"

If he noticed her sarcastic use of "happy", he didn't indicate it. "Within the month, I expect."

"A month isn't very long to organize an event that elaborate," she remarked.

"My mother has enough staff to pull it together in a week," he said dryly. "So should I tell him to make arrangements?"

There was always the possibility he might come to love her in the few weeks leading up to the royal event, but if he didn't…could she take the risk?

"I'd be honored to marry you again in your country because I love you," she said calmly.

"Then all we have to do is choose a date."

"But I won't."

He frowned. "You won't what?"

"I won't do it. I won't go through another ceremony."

His frown deepened. "I don't understand."

She smiled wanly. "I'm more than happy to marry a man I love in any place he chooses and as many times as he would like, but I refuse to marry one for a second time who doesn't love me.

"I'll visit Marestonia, shake hands and kiss babies like any good royal wife. I'll even add Avelogne to the itinerary in order to see my grandmother, but…" she planted both hands on his desk and leaned toward him "…I will *not* listen to your pledge of love and devotion when you don't mean it and are only reciting trite and meaningless words out of duty. How *dare* you even ask me to consider such a thing?"

She straightened. "So tell your father whatever you like to get yourself off the proverbial hook. Say I'm claustrophobic in churches, allergic to flowers, or that lace makes me break out in hives. I don't care what excuse you give, but I will not repeat holy vows with someone who doesn't love me. I have *some* pride and self-respect."

Shaking with indignation and pleased she'd stated her convictions in no uncertain terms, she swept from the room and returned to work.

Dumbfounded, Ruark watched her leave as if she couldn't escape his presence fast enough. Obligations aside, he'd been so sure she would agree because she loved him. He'd only thought of the ceremony as another event to attend, another duty to perform, but clearly Gina had seen the rite as a symbolic, religious act of two people becoming one.

Sheepishly, he admitted he hadn't considered the vows they would make. He'd only focused on how proud he would be to stand beside the woman who made his life complete by the love and laughter she brought.

He'd greedily taken those gifts, never quite expecting or believing his good fortune. Yet, somewhere along the way, she'd become such an integral part of his existence that he couldn't imagine facing a day without her.

In his thoughtlessness and self-centeredness he'd clearly hurt her, and he berated himself for it. He'd rather cut off his right arm than cause Gina pain. He loved her too much to be responsible for giving her a single moment of grief.

Instantly, something broke in his chest, as if he'd finally been released from his chains of denial. He loved her.

Stunned by the revelation, he tried the words on for size again—he loved her!—and realized he meant every word.

He'd always believed he didn't know what love was or how to recognize it, and now he knew he'd been right. He *hadn't* known what true love was because what he'd felt for Grace had been a mere shadow of what he felt for Gina. Love *was* more than affection, companionship, and compatibility. Love implied a passion that went beyond the physical and into the spiritual. It was a desire to spend every moment of the day with an individual, seeing her at her best as well as her worst, and being delighted with each experience.

If this was what Gina felt, then he understood why she had to tell him every chance she could. Others had uttered "I love you" as a throw-away phrase that was useful on occasion, but Gina had spoken it from her heart. How dense he'd been not to recognize the difference and how foolish to let his cynicism rule him. He'd done her a disservice and if she never forgave him for it, she would be justified.

His path suddenly became clear—he had to make amends. He'd call Henri and ask for a special, romantic dinner with candlelight and flowers. No, tonight was too many hours away. He wanted to tell her *now*.

He jumped up, then stopped short. Unfortunately, his meeting with the budget review committee was scheduled to begin in five minutes. He couldn't postpone it without a valid excuse. Needing a private moment with his wife wouldn't carry enough weight to exempt him from the meeting where upper management decided on his department's funding.

Once again duty demanded his attention and he chafed under the obligation, wishing his personal wishes could supersede it once in his life.

It would only be an hour, he consoled himself. Then he would set things straight with the love of his life.

"My gut hurts real bad." The forty-five-year-old truck driver hunched his shoulders forward and rubbed his abdomen. "You gotta do something, Doc."

Gina had already examined the man who answered to Glen "Gibb" Gibson, and hadn't found anything suspicious. Normal-sized liver, no signs of fever or jaundice, normal bowel signs, no spasms, no masses, only tenderness in his right upper quadrant. Palpating his abdomen didn't provide any clues as to why he was experiencing such excruciating pain. Of course, that didn't mean anything, only that whatever was wrong wasn't immediately obvious.

"I'm going to order some bloodwork," she informed him. "I want to check your kidney function as well as your pancreas. Those results should narrow down the possibilities."

Because she still hadn't gotten the lab results from her possible MI patient, she decided to save time and collect the blood samples herself. Within minutes she took Gibb's tubes to the nurses' station and handed them to Lucy.

"I want electrolytes, amylase, CBC, glucose, BUN and creatinine, liver profile, and an acute hepatitis profile," she stated, choosing tests that would give her information about Gibb's kidneys, pancreas, and liver. "Get a urine specimen, too, and find out what happened to my cardiac results."

"Will do." The nurse got on the phone and Gina returned to Gibb's cubicle.

"The tests will take about an hour or so," she informed him. "Meanwhile, we'll collect a urine sample, then send you to X-Ray for abdominal films. After that, we'll let you rest."

She'd scarcely finished when everything happened at once. A loud crash barely registered before the walls and ceiling came crashing down. Instinctively, she tried to cover her head with her arms, but she was too late. Something struck her temple and everything faded to black.

Impatient to finish business so he could leave, Ruark tapped his pen against his copy of the budget proposal. Their discussion was dragging on far too long and at this rate he'd be lucky if they finished their inquisition by noon.

Lansing's secretary bustled in and Ruark bit back a groan. The woman had interrupted twice already and obviously intended to do so again. She passed a note to Dr Lansing who scanned it, then frowned.

"When did this happen?" he asked.

"About ten minutes ago," she answered. "The

phone lines in the ED are down. We just received the news."

Ruark heard "ED" and his whole body went on alert. "What's wrong?"

"You'd better get downstairs," Lansing said grimly. "Someone's just smashed their vehicle into the ER."

Gina.

Ruark didn't hesitate. He bounded for the exit. "Injuries?" he stopped to ask.

"We don't know. Apparently they're still trying to account for everyone. Don't worry, we'll send all available staff to sort out—"

Ruark didn't stay long enough for the chief of medical staff to finish his comment or implement the hospital's internal disaster plan. He bypassed the elevator and ran for the stairs, arriving at his department in record time.

Once he'd pushed his way through the double doors marked "ED Staff Only", the scene reminded him of other disaster sites. Plaster dust hung heavily in the air and at the far end of the hall where patient cubicles had once been, rubble and a half-demolished Humvee now replaced the outer wall and allowed him to see daylight and the visitors' parking lot.

Staff scurried to and fro in organized chaos. Although the damage to the building was extensive and various pieces of wood, steel and brick had been tossed along the entire length of the department from the force of impact, the worst damage was confined to the two treatment rooms where the Humvee had crashed through. Most of the people appeared shaken, but other than a few who were covered in white dust and held towels to their bleeding faces or extremities the number of casualties seemed minimal, their injuries superficial.

"Where's Dr Sutton?" he demanded of a passing male nurse.

"Haven't seen her."

Undamaged rooms held patients and staff, but Gina wasn't to be found. No one remembered where or when they'd seen her last. With dogged determination he continued his search, hoping she'd gone to Radiology or the cafeteria, but his instinct warned him she hadn't.

He found Lucy near the largest pile of rubble, along with another nurse, Hugh and Joachim. Each worked to move the chunks of ceiling and wall.

"Where's Gina?" he demanded, not caring who answered.

Lucy's face was white, her eyes wide with worry as she pointed. "Underneath that. She and her patient are the only ones we can't account for."

Fear beyond anything he'd ever experienced, including the incident with the man pulling a knife, pierced him, but he reined it in as best he could. He had to be calm and objective or he wouldn't do her any good when they finally reached her.

"Find several backboards and a C-spine collar," he commanded the nurse. While she obeyed, he took her place to work alongside his men.

"Your Highness," Hugh said respectfully, "you should step aside and let us handle this."

"Forget it," he snarled. "I'm staying."

He'd made his intentions plain and Hugh simply nodded and returned to work as if he'd known Ruark wouldn't listen.

"It's so amazing," Lucy said, her voice quivering in apparent shock. "We didn't know what had hit us until we saw the Humvee."

"Anyone check the driver?" he asked.

Joachim didn't waste his breath as he heaved another large piece of plaster to the side. "Dead."

"We're thinking he had a heart attack and plowed right in," Lucy huffed as she lifted several smaller pieces of debris out of the way.

"I see an arm," Hugh called out.

Ruark's gut churned, afraid of what he'd find and afraid of what he wouldn't. He wanted to tear through the splintered wood and bricks to reach Gina, but they were playing a game of pick-up-sticks. Unless they worked slowly and methodically to remove each piece, more could come crashing down.

The ceiling tiles had fallen but the braces were still intact, which Ruark considered a good sign. They wouldn't have to shore up the ceiling or worry about the upper floor crashing on top of them.

A few minutes later they'd uncovered Gina and her patient, both buried underneath the wall cabinets that had toppled over them. "Gina?" Ruark called out as they dealt with the unconscious man who lay in front of her.

She didn't answer.

As soon as they'd placed Gina's patient on a stretcher and carted him to a safer location, Ruark knelt beside her.

Gina's groan was like music to his ears. He called her name as he ran his hands over her head and upper body while others worked to free her trapped legs. A lump on her head, a purplish gash along her hairline, cuts and more bruises on her arms, but no broken bones. So far.

"Hurt…everywhere," she murmured.

"I know," he soothed. "We'll have you out in a minute."

It took ten to immobilize her spine, place her on a backboard and carry her into a treatment room as far away from the destruction as possible. "I want X-ray and lab here, as well as a surgeon," Ruark commanded to no one in particular as Lucy began cutting off Gina's shirt.

Seeing she was going into shock, Ruark barked his orders while the nurse started the IV. He leaned over Gina. "Hang in there," he told her.

"I…will. Have…to."

"You're going to be fine," he promised, willing it to be so because he couldn't accept the alternative.

Her mouth twitched as if she was trying to smile. "Won't be…like the…others. Won't…leave you."

"Darned right you won't," he said fiercely. "I love you."

Her eyelids fluttered closed. As he worked frantically to determine how serious the large, darkening bruising across her hips and abdomen was, he was afraid of one thing.

She hadn't heard him.

* * *

For the first time in a number of days, when Gina woke up, she actually felt awake. Tired and worn out, but awake.

Noticing her surroundings—a familiar hospital room—she noticed Ruark sprawled in a nearby chair. She scratched her itchy nose and he sprang out of his seat to stand beside her.

A smile spread across his face until his eyes crinkled. "Good morning, sleepyhead."

She managed a smile. "It doesn't feel like such a good morning."

"You're awake and you're stable. I'd say that's better than good. You've been sedated for several days, you know."

"I didn't realize. No wonder I'm so stiff. I need to sit up." She struggled to find the remote control to raise the head of her bed, but he did the honors.

After she'd settled into a new position, she reached toward his face and stroked his bristly cheek. "You didn't shave," she said inanely.

He clasped her hand and lowered it to his chest. "I spent the night here and haven't gone to the doctors' lounge to change yet. I didn't want to leave you alone."

"Was I that bad?"

He chuckled. "No. I just couldn't go home."

"Why ever not?" she asked. "It isn't like we don't pay our nurses to look after patients."

"True, but I didn't like the idea of you being by yourself. If you had problems, I would have been halfway across town."

"But I didn't have problems," she pointed out.

"Didn't matter. The possibility was there. My parents wanted to fly over as soon as I told them about the accident, including your grandmother, but I told them not to. You see, *I* wanted to be here for you. No one else."

Touched by his statement, she didn't know what to say, so she flexed her aching shoulders and changed the subject. "Are you going to share your diagnosis or do I have to guess?"

"Your liver and kidneys were bruised, but they're healing nicely. We thought we might have to remove your spleen, but Ahmadi decided to wait and see if your blood counts stabilized. So far so good." He grinned. "You also have the usual assortment of scrapes and other bruises, as well as a minor concussion, but it could have been a lot worse."

"My patient? Glen Gibson?"

"Strangely enough, he's in better shape than

you. Probably because you'd managed to push him forward enough so the heaviest pieces fell on you instead. You'll also be interested to know his pancreatitis is coming under control."

"I'm glad. Was anyone else hurt?"

"A few had minor injuries, lacerations and the sort. Other than the driver, you and Gibson were the worst."

"How is he?" she asked.

Ruark shook his head. "Massive coronary. According to his wife, he hadn't felt well but insisted on driving himself to the hospital. It's a shame he didn't listen."

"His family must feel terrible," she said, "but it could have been worse. We could have had a full-blown disaster on our hands."

"It's bad enough," he said. "The ER has been shut down until the engineers can check the structural integrity of our end of the building. Then, once they give the OK, they'll start repairs and we'll be back in business."

"What about the patients?"

"We'll handle what we can through the minor emergency center across the street and route the serious cases to St Bridgit's. In the meantime, staff are temporarily reassigned to different units or they're using their earned time." He grinned. "I'm taking a few days off, too."

"Whatever for?"

"I figure I'll need every one of those days to convince my wife how much I love her."

She froze, wondering if the combination of pain medication and wishful thinking had affected her hearing. "You what?"

He carefully perched on the edge of her bed as he held her hand. "I love you, Gina."

"You… How…? What…? I thought you didn't believe in love."

"I didn't, until you came along. Once I realized how I couldn't imagine a day without you, I knew I was wrong."

Tears welled in her eyes. "I thought…I thought…" Unable to deal with her sudden relief, she began to cry quietly because her muscles were too sore for her to let loose real sobs.

He waited until her emotional storm lightened. "You thought what?"

"I imagined all sorts of possibilities," she confessed, wiping her cheeks with the backs of both hands. "I couldn't decide if you truly didn't love me or were just afraid to say so. Then I thought you'd heard it so many times before from so many other women that you didn't believe me."

"I did believe you, Gina. I just had trouble accepting it. Fool that I was, I thought if I showed you how important you were by my actions, everything would be fine. You'd see how much you meant to me, even if I never said so."

"I tried to tell myself that, but a girl needs to hear the words," she finished simply.

He tipped her chin up. "I didn't do this right the first time, so I'm trying again." He paused. "Will you marry me, Gina? Not because of duty or responsibility, not because of our family history or political expedience, but because I love you?"

Tears threatened again, but they were happy tears. "Oh, yes, I will."

He leaned over and kissed her ever so gently as if afraid she would break.

"Come, now," she teased. "Is that the best you can do?"

"For now," he promised. "I'm saving my best for when you're out of this hospital bed."

She giggled. "Promises, promises."

He grinned down at her. "May I call my father and tell him to organize a wedding?"

"Please, do."

"He'll ask for a date," he warned.

"Tomorrow."

He laughed. "Even my mother can't work that huge a miracle. Besides, you need time to recover. How about a month?"

"Perfect." With her spirits restored, she suddenly wanted to share her mood with everyone. "Do you have your phone with you?"

He pulled it out of the case on his hip. "Yes, why?"

"I'll explain in a minute." Grateful for his international calling plan, she scrolled through his contact list to find the name she wanted.

"I can call for you," he began.

"I know, but this is something I have to do myself." After pressing a button, she waited... The number she'd dialed began ringing and a woman answered.

Her crisp accent reminded her so much of her parents' that Gina could hardly speak past the lump in her throat, but somehow she managed.

"Grandmother?" she croaked. "It's me. Gina..."

EPILOGUE

"MY BROTHER would have been so proud to see this day," King Henrik stated as he threaded Gina's arm through his in the vestibule of St Gregory's Cathedral in the heart of Marestonia's capital city.

"I think so, too." She smiled at her uncle, who resembled her father so closely it was uncanny. "Thank you for giving me away."

"It's my honor and privilege." The twinkle in his eyes belied his solemn expression. "I'll be glad when it's over, though," he said. "Planning a royal wedding in less than a month, even a small one like yours, has turned both palaces upside down. Your aunt and grandmother discussed nothing but fabrics and dress designs for days. I can't imagine what Ruark's parents went through to organize their end."

While tradition required the bride marry in her family seat, she and Ruark chose to spread the celebration between both countries in order to avoid slighting anyone. They'd opted to hold the actual ceremony and reception in Marestonia, with her uncle giving her away in lieu of her father. The formal wedding ball would follow in Avelogne.

"I know, and I'm sorry for all the problems I caused."

He patted her hand. "Nonsense, my dear. This event was what everyone needed. It's a shame you'll be returning to America so soon. We haven't had nearly enough time to talk."

"We'll come back to visit," she promised.

Gina could hardly hear the music over the pounding of her heart. She knew the flower girls were slowly scattering the rose petals along the white-carpeted center aisle as they'd practiced during last night's rehearsal. In a few minutes the wedding co-ordinators would cue her uncle and it would be her turn.

While she waited, she fingered the ivory-colored handkerchief that had been in her family for generations and had once been framed and hung in a place of honor in her parents' bedroom. Ten names had been embroidered on it so far, and as part of their tradition Gina's name had been added underneath her mother's. Someday her daughter's name would appear there as well.

Buoyed by the thought of Ruark waiting for her, her jitters faded as the orchestra began playing the *Lohengren*'s Bridal Chorus. "This is your last opportunity to run out the back door," Henrik joked.

"We're already married, so it's not an option," she reminded him with a smile.

The aisle seemed to stretch for miles, but she focused on Ruark as he waited for her in the sanctuary, looking distinguished in his official state regalia with all the accoutrements of his royal family. He might already be her legal husband, but today he would become the husband of her heart.

Her uncle placed her hand in Ruark's, then stepped back while Ruark took his place at her side.

He whispered over the chamber ensemble's performance. "You look beautiful."

"So do you."

"I thought you'd never get here."

"I walked as fast as I could. We didn't have to do this, you know."

"And deny everyone all this excitement? They would never have forgiven us."

For all the fuss and uproar, Gina knew both

families had been thrilled by their decision and members of both royal houses had pitched in to help. She'd been more than grateful because she didn't care about flowers, colors, music, or the food. She was only interested in repeating her vows because this time they would both mean them.

As the music began to fade, she teased, "Does His Royal Highness have any final comments before he marries his wife again?"

He squeezed her hand tightly. "How does 'I love you' sound?"

"Perfect. Absolutely perfect."

MEDICAL™

Large Print

Titles for the next six months…

September

THE CHILDREN'S DOCTOR'S SPECIAL PROPOSAL	Kate Hardy
ENGLISH DOCTOR, ITALIAN BRIDE	Carol Marinelli
THE DOCTOR'S BABY BOMBSHELL	Jennifer Taylor
EMERGENCY: SINGLE DAD, MOTHER NEEDED	Laura Iding
THE DOCTOR CLAIMS HIS BRIDE	Fiona Lowe
ASSIGNMENT: BABY	Lynne Marshall

October

A FAMILY FOR HIS TINY TWINS	Josie Metcalfe
ONE NIGHT WITH HER BOSS	Alison Roberts
TOP-NOTCH DOC, OUTBACK BRIDE	Melanie Milburne
A BABY FOR THE VILLAGE DOCTOR	Abigail Gordon
THE MIDWIFE AND THE SINGLE DAD	Gill Sanderson
THE PLAYBOY FIREFIGHTER'S PROPOSAL	Emily Forbes

November

THE SURGEON SHE'S BEEN WAITING FOR	Joanna Neil
THE BABY DOCTOR'S BRIDE	Jessica Matthews
THE MIDWIFE'S NEW-FOUND FAMILY	Fiona McArthur
THE EMERGENCY DOCTOR CLAIMS HIS WIFE	Margaret McDonagh
THE SURGEON'S SPECIAL DELIVERY	Fiona Lowe
A MOTHER FOR HIS TWINS	Lucy Clark

™ MILLS & BOON®

MEDICAL™

Large Print

December

THE GREEK BILLIONAIRE'S LOVE-CHILD	Sarah Morgan
GREEK DOCTOR, CINDERELLA BRIDE	Amy Andrews
THE REBEL SURGEON'S PROPOSAL	Margaret McDonagh
TEMPORARY DOCTOR, SURPRISE FATHER	Lynne Marshall
DR VELASCOS' UNEXPECTED BABY	Dianne Drake
FALLING FOR HER MEDITERRANEAN BOSS	Anne Fraser

January

THE VALTIERI MARRIAGE DEAL	Caroline Anderson
THE REBEL AND THE BABY DOCTOR	Joanna Neil
THE COUNTRY DOCTOR'S DAUGHTER	Gill Sanderson
SURGEON BOSS, BACHELOR DAD	Lucy Clark
THE GREEK DOCTOR'S PROPOSAL	Molly Evans
SINGLE FATHER: WIFE AND MOTHER WANTED	Sharon Archer

February

EMERGENCY: WIFE LOST AND FOUND	Carol Marinelli
A SPECIAL KIND OF FAMILY	Marion Lennox
HOT-SHOT SURGEON, CINDERELLA BRIDE	Alison Roberts
A SUMMER WEDDING AT WILLOWMERE	Abigail Gordon
MIRACLE: TWIN BABIES	Fiona Lowe
THE PLAYBOY DOCTOR CLAIMS HIS BRIDE	Janice Lynn

™ MILLS & BOON®